What Readers are Saying

About *The Karma Murders:*

"I loved, loved, loved *The Karma Murders*, the second book in the *Gabrieli Mysteries*. It felt like going back home. Love Gabe, love the ensemble cast, the new additions, everything. As usual, Gabe's private life is a bit of a mess, but that doesn't keep him from recognizing foul play when he stumbles across it—and then doing something about it."

Marcelle Dubé, award-winning author of *The Mendenhall Mysteries* and *The All'e Chronicles*

About *The End Game:*

"…just the beginning to an addictive new series."

Robert Dugoni, New York Times Best Selling Author of *The Tracy Crosswhite Series.*

THE KARMA MURDERS

A Gabrieli Mystery

CHARLOTTE MORGANTI

HALFDAN
PRESS

For Kobbie,

Who has been with Gabe Gabrieli since the moment he first parked his F150 on Main Street in Cheakamus, B.C.

June 2010
TRUCK STOP PARKING LOT NEAR
CHEAKAMUS, BRITISH COLUMBIA

Leonard Wurtz leaned out the driver's side window of the Winnebago and accepted the two go-cups from the hitchhiker. "There's a black coffee for your wife and the hot chocolate with whip you wanted," the fellow said. "Hope you enjoy it."

Leonard handed his wife her drink and then tasted his own. "Mmmm, yum." He shook raindrops from his sleeve. "We appreciate the drinks, but you didn't have to do this. It's a crappy night, and we were happy to give you a lift." He drank deeply from his cup.

The man peered from beneath his Australian bush hat and smiled. "You saved me from a wet hike up the highway."

Leonard chugged more of his hot chocolate. "You sure you don't want to continue on down the road with us?"

As a car pulled into the lot, the man ducked his head and shielded his eyes from the headlights with his hand. "No, thanks." He waved and backed away. "I'll be going. Safe travels now."

"Hey, hang on," Leonard said. He drained his cup and then held it out the window. "Do me a favor and toss this cup in the bin over there? Thanks again. Safe travels yourself."

Monday, July 12, 2010
CHEAKAMUS, BRITISH COLUMBIA

GABE GABRIELI EXITED HIS F150, smacked the button on the wall to lower the garage overhead door, and climbed the interior stairs to his apartment as quickly as his tender knee would allow. He had fifteen minutes before he was due for his afternoon shift at The Peak Bar. He needed ten of those minutes to ensure that when he walked into the bar, he didn't look like a person who'd just lost a wrestling contest with a steer. Which he had.

As soon as he pushed the apartment door open, he heard a soft thud and a petulant yowl. A ginger cat appeared in the bedroom doorway, paused with one paw raised, and studied Gabe as he would an unknown alien.

"Hey Doofus, did you have a good day?"

The cat yowled again and paced to his bowl on the kitchen floor. There he sat, staring at Gabe.

"Yeah, yeah, I know. Food. Do you think of anything except food and sleep?"

Doofus squinted, then lifted a hind leg and tended to his nether regions.

"Oh, right. I forgot. Food, sleep, and clean privates."

Gabe opened a cupboard door in the kitchen and

extracted two tins of moist cat food. He held the first one out to Doofus. "Beef and real gravy?" The cat blinked.

Gabe held out the second tin. "Chicken?" Doofus arched his back and hissed.

"Right," Gabe said, opening the tin of beef and gravy. "Beef's your favorite, hey? A true Albertan."

After he emptied the food into the cat's bowl, Gabe changed into a clean pair of jeans and a black turtleneck sweater. Before he pulled on his boots, he brushed them to remove evidence that he'd been dragged through the dirt and steer dung in O'Malley's stockade.

Doofus wove his body around and between Gabe's ankles, purring.

"Happy, buddy?" Gabe scratched the cat's head.

He grabbed his keys and headed out the door. When his knee protested as he descended the stairs, he took a moment to massage the tender joint. Who would have thought that being dragged across the arena could bang a guy up so much? Surely this wasn't a sign he was aging.

———

Shortly after two o'clock Gabe's business partner and best friend, Harris Chilton, entered through the main doors of The Peak Bar. Stan Wurtz and Wally Mitchell followed behind.

Gabe took a second look at the trio as they approached. Harris and Wally flanked Stan and appeared ready to grab him if he stumbled. Usually, Stan moved with quick energy. Usually, a grin creased his face. Usually, he greeted everyone with a loud "Hiya! How ya doon?"

Now he shuffled across the floor, his face was somber, and his "hiya" as he slid onto a bar stool was subdued. The last time Gabe had seen Stan this down was at his parents' memorial service in June, over a month ago.

"Hey Stan," Gabe said, "what's going on? You don't look so great."

Stan's skin had a gray cast to it, and his eyes watered. He swiped at his eyes and said, "I heard from Sergeant LeBlanc this morning. About Mom and Dad."

Paul LeBlanc was a sergeant in the RCMP detachment in Trail, a city an hour down the highway from Cheakamus.

Stan continued. "Their Winnebago checked out okay mechanically, although he said it was hard to be certain since it was totaled from the wreck." Stan's smile was bitter. "Plummeting off the side of a mountain will do that to an RV. Pour me a draft okay?"

Last June, Leonard and Verna Wurtz, Stan's parents, left for a much needed and long-awaited vacation on Vancouver Island. The same trip they'd taken every year for the last twenty years. Except this time Leonard apparently lost control of their RV on a steep decline. The Wurtzes both died when the vehicle plunged into a rocky ravine.

"Then it really was an accident?" Gabe said, as he placed Stan's pint on the bar.

Stan clutched at his hair. "I don't give a damn what the official decision is. Dad was a careful driver. It's ludicrous to think he'd drive off the side of a mountain!"

"Maybe he swerved to avoid an animal on the road," Gabe said. "Weird things happen."

Harris said, "Stan, tell Gabe what else LeBlanc told you."

Stan sipped his beer and then took a deep breath. "LeBlanc is a thorough guy. While they were checking out the RV, and before they released Mom and Dad's bodies to me, he got the coroner or whoever does this stuff to take a bunch of blood samples. And guess what? Dad's tox screen showed traces of a sedative."

Stan stabbed his index finger toward Gabe. "Dad never, *never,* took sedatives. Never! So that proves it. Someone killed my parents."

Okay, that was strange. Who would want to kill two retirees who loved bingo? And volunteered at the wildlife rescue center? "That's terrible, Stan. However, it *is* good news in a weird way. Not that someone killed your parents. But that they found evidence. LeBlanc and his team will trace the sedative, find out who might have bought it. If someone slipped it to your father, they can probably find out who did it and why."

Stan stared at him and slowly shook his head. "Nope. They won't do any of that."

"That doesn't sound right."

Stan raised his eyebrows. "Apparently my father could have taken something the day before the crash, which could have still been in his system when he got behind the wheel. A trace isn't enough to prove anything. Apparently."

"That doesn't sound like LeBlanc," Gabe said. In fact, the whole story seemed bizarre.

Harris chimed in. "It's not LeBlanc, it's his second in command. This guy says the drug could have made its way into Leonard's system in any number of innocent ways. Without evidence of injection or some other interference with Leonard's body, he's not willing to look further."

"Yeah," Stan said. "Sergeant LeBlanc is in Toronto for some boondoggle. He's not able to oversee any case from there and has assigned general command of the detachment to Corporal Lightheart. More like Corporal Lightbrain."

Gabe poured himself glass of water and took a sip. "Could Lightheart be right? Could there be an innocent explanation for what happened?"

Stan shook his head rapidly. "I told you, Gabe. No way my dad would take a sedative! Not knowingly. He did that a few years ago, took one of my mom's pills. Instead of making him sleep, it gave him waking hallucinations. He swore he'd never touch something like that again."

"Did you tell Lightheart that?"

"Oh yeah. He asked for proof. How was I gonna prove that? It's not like Dad filmed himself hallucinating. So, no proof for the idiot cop."

Stan shook his head, took a breath, and sipped his beer. "At least no proof so far. Lightheart turned over everything they found in the RV in addition to their suitcases and the contents of the fridge. One map, two gas receipts, one takeout cup, one tire gauge. Even a green sticky note with the word 'karma' scrawled on it, which they found in the pocket on the back of the driver's seat. But no pills."

"Did they test that cup?" Gabe asked.

"According to Lightheart, yes. It was clean. He said he doesn't have enough to justify keeping the file open." Stan sneered. "And you know, they are a busy detachment, and they have criminals to catch."

Wally Mitchell, who'd been listening silently to the conversation, said, "Your parents were just about the nicest people going. When I got swindled in that mining scam years ago and went a bit off the rails, they were very kind to me. Two of a handful of people in town who treated me like a normal person. Then when my wife left me because of it all, your mom brought me casseroles."

Stan laughed. "Yeah, that was Mom. Casseroles fixed everything, she believed."

"So, like I said, nicest people going," Wally continued. "I can't see anyone wanting to kill them. Of course you don't want to believe it was an accident, but ask yourself. Who'd want to kill them? I mean really?"

Stan drained his beer. He slid off his stool and paced. His voice rose. "Why does there have to be a reason? How about some maniac out there? Remember years ago when that retired couple in their RV went missing? And the vehicle turned up, burned to a crisp? Or how about the guy in Arizona who killed a couple in their trailer because he wanted the food in their fridge? What if the guy simply hates RVs and the people in them? Maybe the vehicle triggers brain waves that tell him to kill the alien invaders. Who knows why something happens?"

The three of them stared at Stan. He raked his hand through his hair. "Okay, rant over. Thanks for listening. If the cops won't pursue it, that doesn't mean I can't. I'll look through their papers and see if I can find something other than stupid sticky notes. Perhaps something was going on that I didn't pay attention to."

He jutted his chin toward Gabe. "And if I strike out, I'll bring in a hired gun. Assuming Gabe's calendar isn't already full." Not waiting for an answer, Stan waved goodbye and headed to the door.

Gabe cleared Stan's mug from the bar. Strange about the tox screen.

Monday, July 12, 2010
THE PEAK BAR

A FEW MINUTES after Stan left, the outer door of The Peak Bar burst open and slammed against the wall, momentarily deafening Gabe. It was either a police raid, or Maxine Lanning.

Gabe glanced over his shoulder. Maxine stood in the doorway and surveyed the bar, one hand raised to catch the door as it rebounded off the wall.

A take-no-prisoners journalist, recently transplanted from Vancouver, Maxine had purchased *The Journal*, the local paper, from Bill Jacobson six months ago. The official reason Bill had sold was that he wanted to retire to Arizona. A cynic would say Bill moved away because his reputation took a beating last fall when he launched a smear campaign against both Gabe and people Gabe cared about. When the town rallied behind Gabe, Bill found it advisable to head for warmer climes.

"Hey guys," Maxine said as she strode up to the bar. She wore a tank top and jeans. Her auburn hair swung behind her head in a loose ponytail. The new owner of *The Journal* was an ethical reporter and fun to be around. Everything Bill Jacobson was not. Whether it was her rocket-scientist intelligence, or her wicked wit, Gabe didn't know. Didn't care either. She added spice to the stew.

"Max, hi. Want your usual?" Gabe reached for the house red.

"Oh no, I'm here on official business, and that means no booze. I was going through Jacobson's archives. I found a series of articles he wrote about you. They had to do with some trouble you had with the police in Calgary. Is there a story there you want to talk about?"

Gabe folded his arms as he leaned against the back counter. "No."

"Oh, come on. It's a slow news week here. I thought I could run a little retrospective on you. In fact, I'm going to make it a monthly column—looking back at some of the town's more colorful citizens. What do you say?"

Gabe furrowed his brow. His jaw clenched. "No."

She pursed her lips and blew out a breath. "Here's the thing. Besides looking at the archives, I did some research. Something we journalists are good at. I could write a gripping story about a man who died in Calgary not so long ago and how you got yourself all muddled up in the middle of it and ended up in jail, and how Harris here saved you from what I think would have been a lengthy sentence. That is, of course, if the case had gone to trial and if the jury had seen things the cops' way. But I hate printing only one side of things. That's why I'm asking nicely if you want to tell me what really happened."

Harris and Wally Mitchell traded looks.

Gabe stared at Maxine, unsmiling. Spice could be over-done. First, Bill Jacobson had been on Gabe's case about his Calgary past. Now it was Maxine. Nothing changed. No one was prepared to let the past die. So long as the cloud of Drake's death hung over Gabe's head, people would wonder, wanting to know if, maybe, just maybe, he really had killed Drake. If maybe, just maybe, Harris had run a fast one, conned the courts, got his buddy out of a jam through subterfuge.

Part of him wanted to tell her to take her journalistic interest and shove it. He was tired of people poking into that part of his life. Another part of him, however, wanted Maxine to know the truth. He was tired of people being afraid of him, worrying whether he was a violent man. The need to make her understand won out.

Gabe sipped his water. "I'm not saying anything on the record. Still want my side of things?"

"I'd be an idiot if I said no," Maxine said. "Off the record, it is."

Gabe turned to Harris and Wally. "You've heard this before, so I won't be offended if you fall asleep."

Harris grinned. "Heck, I love hearing how I was the knight who charged in to save your sorry butt. It's energizing."

Wally nodded. "Me too."

"Okay Max, here's the short version, off the record. My wife Bethany is a TV news anchor. She attracted a stalker named Andover Drake. This was when we were still married and living near Calgary. Well, we're still married, but not together, I mean. Anyway, I made the mistake of finding Drake and pounding his ass. Told him to leave Beth the hell alone or I'd fix him. Of course, he turns up dead and I'm arrested. Things were looking disastrous for a while until Harris rode in on his white charger and saved the day. He proved the cops didn't have any evidence other than my big mouth. The charges were dropped."

"Who really killed the guy?" Maxine asked.

"Dunno. I spent some time trying to find out. The whole thing— beating up Drake, the murder charge, the court hearing—destroyed my life. Beth took a year-long assignment to Europe. My legal practice cratered. The Law Society got on my case. Harris had to make another trip to Calgary and drag me out of the gutter."

Harris said, "The least I could do for my lifelong best friend."

Gabe put his glass into the dishwasher under the bar. "Every now and then, I look at the case again. Because once you've been charged with murder, no one really believes you didn't do it, until someone else is caught. If I can find out who killed Drake, I can get the dirt off my name." He cocked his head at Maxine and grimaced. "Really, Max, the whole thing is old news, and I'd like to keep it that way."

She studied him for a long moment. "So, here's an idea. When you find the stalker's killer, let me have first dibs on the story."

"Depends on whether Hollywood offers me a better deal."

She stared at him. "Are you kidding me?"

Gabe shrugged. "Maybe. Maybe not."

"Hah!"

"If you're looking for something other than old news," Harris said to Maxine, "you should talk to Stan Wurtz about the tox screen they ran on his father."

"What?"

"Stan believes there's some question whether the accident that killed his parents was actually an accident."

"What do you think, Gabe?" Maxine asked.

"There are some unanswered questions, for sure."

Monday, July 12, 2010
TIFFANY'S CAFÉ, CHEAKAMUS, B.C.

As soon as his shift ended at six o'clock, Gabe limped across Main Street to Tiffany's Café. One of the two social hubs of Cheakamus (The Peak Bar being the second), Rhonda Zalesko's diner had been his go-to place for almost every meal since last October when he first arrived in town.

When he entered the café, he inhaled the aromas coming from the kitchen—roast something, for sure. And a spice he couldn't identify, which was no surprise since Gabe recognized only the smell of BBQ sauce. If forced, he'd admit BBQ sauce wasn't a spice per se, but it was the only seasoning item in his own kitchen besides salt, pepper, ketchup and Dijon mustard.

He studied the chalkboard hanging on the wall behind the counter, where Rhonda listed the daily special in her spikey script. "Island Pork."

Gabe was conflicted. Whatever concoction Rhonda had christened "Island Pork" was new, at least to him. And the name didn't tell him what ingredients the dish contained, besides pork. If he ordered the special, would she bring a whole piglet to his booth, complete with the de rigueur apple? Would he have to stare at the tiny thing's sad eyes before digging in? Or worse, would the piglet be adorned with pineapple? He shuddered.

"Oh, for heaven's sake," Gabe's Goody-Two-Shoes side said. "When has Rhonda messed up with food? Almost never. Live on the wild side, why don't you?"

Gabe nodded to himself. Rhonda was an excellent chef. If he ignored the time she served meatloaf for almost a week straight, she hadn't taken a misstep in the kitchen ever.

Tiffany's was hopping—two-thirds full of locals and sprinkled here and there with summer tourists. Gabe grabbed a menu from the front counter as he walked past, heading for his favorite booth at the back, near the jukebox. As usual, it was available. Not because people left it vacant for him, but because it was at the back of the café, by the entrance to the hallway and the bathrooms. One of the toilets in the men's room screeched like a banshee whenever it was flushed, making conversations in Gabe's chosen booth a chore. But since he liked to eat more than talk when he was in Tiffany's, this was the perfect setup.

Gabe barely had a moment to sit down before a tall, gangly server appeared.

"Hey, Owen," Gabe said.

The kid's Adam's apple jerked up and down. "Hi, Mr. Gabrieli."

Gabe studied Owen while he waited for him to describe tonight's special. Perhaps a year or two older than Gabe's kid brother, Jack. So, nineteen, twenty. A nose as prominent as his Adam's apple, pale skin, a heartbreakingly skimpy attempt at a mustache. Gabe knew there was more to Owen than appeared on the surface. He hung around with Rhonda's kids and Jack. That told Gabe Owen had a personality. He evidently hid it well at work.

Owen stood there for a long moment, staring back at Gabe, and then seemed to remember his role in their interaction. He flushed crimson and pulled a cheat sheet from his apron pocket. "Ahhh, tonight our special is pork tenderloin island style. Made with chef's famous secret seasonings." He paused and consulted the sheet once more. "Deserving of a feature in Food Stars Magazine. Succulent, spicy, and decadent. To die for. Mon."

"Did Rhonda write up that description?"

The hint of a smile appeared on Owen's face. "Hmmm. Yes, Mrs. Zalesko, um, Chef Rhonda, does all the descriptions."

Gabe tapped the menu. "Anything in here you'd recommend over the special?"

"No sir. I tasted the special, and it is fantastic." Owen paused for a beat. "To die for, mon." He grinned at Gabe.

"Hah! Okay," Gabe said, "you sold me. And I'll get myself a coffee."

When Owen left, Gabe rose from the booth and entered the men's room. He reached under the counter and retrieved a laminated "out-of-order" sign he'd hidden there weeks ago. He touched the double-sided tape on the back of the sign. "Good to go."

He slapped the sign on the banshee toilet's stall.

After exiting the men's room, he stopped by the rack of coffee thermoses under the antique mirror midway down the café's center aisle. Scrawled on the mirror was a list of "Today's Oso Negro Beans." Gabe didn't need to look far to make his selection. Prince of Darkness, his most recent standby, had top billing on the list.

Aware of the twinges in his knee and the overly full mug of coffee, Gabe walked slowly back to the booth. Setting his mug down, he slid onto the seat and tried not to scream when he bumped his knee against the table support.

When Owen delivered his meal, the aroma was heady, conjuring images of white sand beaches and turquoise water. Gabe's mouth watered. The first time he'd tasted Rhonda's cooking, he'd asked her to marry him. She had refused, perhaps sensing that his proposal was self-serving. Perhaps because she was happily married to a long-haul trucker. Then Gabe asked her to adopt him. "Hah," Rhonda had said, "got two kids already, not looking for more."

However, her refusal to marry or adopt him didn't stop Gabe from sitting in the back booth at Tiffany's almost every evening. Boycotting her café would hurt him more than her.

He attacked the special. Owen's description was bang on. Island Pork was to die for.

By the time Gabe had devoured his dinner, the café had emptied significantly. Rhonda came by, carrying a fresh mug of coffee for him and a glass of water for herself. She slid onto the opposite seat. "What have you done to yourself this time?" she asked.

"Huh?"

"You were limping when you came in. A sure sign you've had your usual interaction with physical activity."

He could have told Rhonda the Frikkin Comedian, the bête noire who loved to mess with his life, had shown up when he was attempting to wrestle a steer. But he had his pride. A half-truth would do. "I was at Seamus O'Malley's ranch, helping with the herd."

"Helping. Right. Playing rodeo, more likely. So, what was it this time?"

"Steers. I don't think Seamus trains them right because they don't pay attention to the rules. Steers are supposed to stop when a guy grabs their horns. Especially when the guy's from Alberta and grew up around rodeos. But noooo, O'Malley's steers just keep running, dragging a fellow's sorry butt along with them."

"Kee-ryste, Gabe," Rhonda said, rolling her eyes. "Just because you wear boots and jeans, and know how to ride a horse, doesn't mean you're a cow hand. What, are you going to enter the rodeo circuit next? Leave that stuff to the young ones."

Gabe sputtered. "Young ones? I'm not even forty yet. In fact, forty is a way off."

Rhonda's face changed, her wide grin replaced by a wistful look. "Ah, yes, forty. I wish." Then she straightened in her seat, smacked the tabletop with her hands and said, "Something I want to kick around with you."

"What's up?"

"Do you know we have over five thousand residents now? I think your god-daughter Devon was citizen number five thousand and one. And you became five thousand and two last year, when you decided to stay."

"Huh. Pretty soon, Cheakamus will be more than a blip on the map."

Rhonda went on. "The thing about the population is this —the town must now either contract directly with the RCMP, instead of letting the province cover the costs, or set up our own police force. Those of us on the town council are leaning toward our own force."

"Uh-huh."

"So how about you become our Chief of Police? Trade your part-time private investigator status, which probably doesn't pay for cat food, for the cushy position and solid salary of top cop."

Gabe squinted at Rhonda. He took a sip of coffee and placed his mug carefully on the tabletop. "Have you been smoking something, Rhonda?"

"No. Why?"

"You're talking gibberish."

"I guess that's a no, then? Okay, if you won't take the top cop job, who do you think we should recruit?"

"LeBlanc."

Rhonda smiled ruefully. "My first thought too. But I heard a rumor our favorite Mountie is leaving town. I think they're shipping him east."

"Maybe if you offer him the job of Police Chief, he'll turn

down the transfer. I bet there are days when LeBlanc wants to take it easy. Trade the stress of heading an RCMP detachment for the laid-back job of policing a tiny peace-loving municipality where trouble is a four-letter word."

Rhonda raised her eyebrows at Gabe. "Where would that utopia be?"

———

When Gabe arrived home, the sun was slipping behind Rimrock Mountain to the west, shooting streaks of fire across the sky in a see-you-tomorrow message. Streetlights had just illuminated and cast a warm glow over the town. He stood at his balcony slider and gazed at the view. During the winter, this view of Cheakamus often reminded him of a Krieghoff painting. Tonight, however, the colors in the sky were more reminiscent of Ted Harrison's landscapes.

Cheakamus *was* a utopia. Except perhaps, to Stan Wurtz who, because of his father's tox results, was convinced his parents' accident was suspicious. But did a person ever really know someone else? Even a loved one? Everyone had secrets.

When The Helper Was Five
TRAIL, B.C.

THE BOY HEARD the crunch of gravel as a vehicle pulled into the driveway. He abandoned his game of fetch with the Blue Heeler and ran around the house to the front lawn. Mommy's dusty and dented pickup sat there, its driver's door wide open.

Mommy was here to take him home!

He raced to the back of the house, collected his stuffy Tigger, and opened the back door to the kitchen. As he stepped inside, he heard Auntie Ann (who wasn't really his aunt, but Mommy said to call her that) say, "Louise! You've been crying. I guess that means bad news?"

Mommy said, "Seven years. Seven!"

"Omigod," Auntie said. "What are you going to do?"

Mommy sagged onto a wooden kitchen chair, put her face in her hands, and wailed. The boy's bottom lip quivered. He didn't like it when mommy was sad. In between her sobs, he heard "Ontario." Mommy blew her nose and then said, "It's not fair, Ann."

Auntie said, "Well, he did take that money."

Mommy sucked in a big breath, a sign the boy knew meant she was angry.

"That's a damn lie!" Mommy said. "You're just like the rest of them. Out to get him. Ruining our lives for the fun of it."

Tuesday, July 13, 2010
TIFFANY'S CAFÉ, CHEAKAMUS

At five-thirty Tuesday morning, lights burned in three businesses along Main Street of Cheakamus. The first was Jerry's Flapjacks and Lounge, which catered to the late-night drinkers and the early-rising truckers. Second was *The Journal*, the town newspaper. And third was Tiffany's Café, famous for more than breakfast. Rhonda Zalesko, the café's owner, stood in front of the open shelves in the cooler, arms akimbo. "Shit, shit, shit, how stupid can I be?"

Eggs. A simple thing to remember. But did she write it down? Nope. Did she remember to buy them when she went to the grocery store last night? Nope. "Shit, shit, shit."

She grabbed the eggs that were in the cooler. About three dozen, she guessed. That would get her through the first hour of the breakfast rush. Maybe. Or she could use them for cakes and pie pastry. Where was her head these days? Why couldn't she remember the simplest thing? Frank had begun teasing her lately. "Is it true the mind is the first to go?" he'd ask when she'd neglected to do something or forgotten a conversation he insisted they'd had only a week ago.

She moved to the work counter in the kitchen and caught sight of her reflection in the café windows. It was the middle of summer and yet still so dark outside that the windows became a mirror. Summer in the mountains—dark as ink until well after seven or eight in the morning. And according to Gabe Gabrieli, what passed for a sunrise here was nothing compared to the "real" sunrises he'd known growing up in the prairies.

She ducked her head to avoid her reflection. Better to focus on cooking than an image that confirmed she looked as old as she felt.

She stared at the eggs on the counter. How could the day be in the tank before it even started? She had promised herself this day would be a typical take-charge day. But now, she didn't know where to start. Save the eggs for the breakfast crowd? Or get the day's baking started?

It wasn't like she had the luxury of time. She knew that, in an hour and a half, Tiffany's door would open twice in rapid succession. The first entrants would be Etta Clayton and her brother Nestor, delivering the day's supply of muffins. One of the best things Rhonda had done was sign Etta to an exclusive contract for muffins. They were almost as famous as Tiffany's and could not be purchased anywhere else in town. Not even if you talked sweet to Etta.

Second across the threshold would be Maxine Lanning, the new owner of *The Journal*. Maxine delivered copies of the newspaper at seven o'clock precisely every Wednesday and Saturday. The other days of the week she arrived at the same time, looking for a muffin, a coffee, and a bit of conversation with Rhonda. They'd become close friends in the six months since Maxine took over the paper.

Etta and Maxine were two of the women in town who had saved Rhonda's bacon more times than she could remember. And now, the light finally went on. Etta would hopefully save not only Rhonda's bacon, but her eggs today. Etta would be long awake and hard at work in her kitchen, so it was safe to phone her, which Rhonda did.

"Etta, hi it's Rhonda. Listen, can you spot me some eggs? I forgot to buy some last night. I need about four dozen, but I'll take what you can spare."

When Etta said she had plenty of eggs and would bring them along with today's muffins, Rhonda punched the air with her fist. She could use the eggs she had on hand to get a start on the baking for the day. The first crisis of the day was averted.

Rhonda pulled the ground beef from the refrigerator. Meatloaf. Today, which looked like it was going to be a botch-up of a day, an anxious day at the very least, called for comfort food and that called for meatloaf. As she kneaded the mixture of beef, eggs, breadcrumbs, and seasonings, she relaxed.

Comfort food used to mean mac and cheese, but that was when her children, David and Roxanne, were small. Mac and cheese fixed everything then. Made the kids love her and want to be at home with her, made her feel like a successful mom. Now the kids were teens and too grown up for mac and cheese.

Rhonda portioned the meatloaf mixture into six loaf pans, enough for the dinner rush and perhaps meatloaf sandwiches tomorrow for the food bank's lunch program. Next, pies.

———

By six-thirty, Rhonda had pastry for ten pies chilling in the fridge. She leaned against the center island, yawned and closed her eyes. Her legs ached, her eyes stung, and her back hurt. If only she could sleep.

She felt like she was doing it all by herself. Frank took longer and longer routes to keep the trucking business going. It was hard to find reliable drivers who were willing to do the long hauls. The drivers Frank hired were mostly young guys who said they had to help raise their kids. Hah. That wasn't an option when she and Frank were raising babies. Twenty years ago, a man's freedom to help with child-rearing was reserved for the wealthy who didn't need to work tough jobs like trucking.

"You're a strong woman, lover," Frank constantly told her. "I never worry about you here in Cheakamus while I'm on the road. I know you can handle whatever this rinky-dink town hands you."

She'd fooled even him.

It wasn't only Frank who saw her as invincible. Most people in town thought she was an in-charge, take-charge type of person. Calm, assured, rational. If they only knew the nights she lay awake fretting, the anxiety she felt whenever things looked to be going sideways, the times she talked to herself in the car and called herself stupid. It was all smoke and mirrors, really. She wasn't strong. She was a fake, a fraud, and it was only a matter of time before everyone figured that out.

The nights were the worst. If she didn't get to sleep as soon as her head hit the pillow, she spent hours fretting. About the kids. The state of the world. Whales with bellies full of plastic. Abandoned animals. Homeless families.

Without warning, the heat appeared—creeping up her neck and making her cheeks burn. Her clothes stuck to her and her forehead felt sticky. This was at least the eighth spell she'd had in the last month. Some were fleeting, some longer —heat rising and enveloping her body unexpectedly, and for no reason. Jesus, she was only forty-two. Surely that was too young for menopause. Not only did her memory seem to be going, but her reproductive parts as well. Not that she wanted any more children, she just didn't want to lose the part of her that made her youthful—the ability to bear children. Silly perhaps, but that's the way she thought of it. The ability to conceive defined "not yet over the hill" and she really did not want to be over that particular hill.

After a few minutes, the heat dissipated, and she shivered as her body cooled. She should go see a doctor. Rhonda shook her head. No, that was not something she felt up to doing yet. She didn't want to face whatever news the doctor might give her. "Just add it to the list of things you fret about every night," she told herself.

6

Tuesday, July 13, 2010
THE PEAK BAR

THE PEAK BAR was unusually quiet Tuesday afternoon. A solitary drinker in the back corner of the bar sipped his draft and stared at his laptop screen. A trio of mountain bikers occupied one of the tables along the far wall, discussing their latest excursion on the trail leading from Deception Ridge into River Flats. The stools pulled up to the bar itself were empty. The most frenzied activity in the room was the dancing of the dust motes in the beams of the strong summer sun coming through the windows.

Harris, who co-owned the bar with Gabe and Gabe's sister Lucy, had disappeared into the office at the back of the bar to work on payroll. John Smith, a recent high school grad from down east who Gabe had hired to operate the bar's kitchen and help with drink orders, delivered menus to the mountain bikers.

Gabe smiled when he heard Smitty waxing poetic over The Peak's burgers and poutine. Even though he was an Anglo, Smitty pronounced "poutine" the way Quebecers did: **poo**-tseen. The bikers exchanged confused glances, and then Smitty repeated the word the Anglo way: poo-**teen**. "Oh, yeah!" one of the trio said. "However you pronounce it, I love that stuff."

When Smitty disappeared into the kitchen with the food orders from the mountain bikers, Gabe loaded dirty pint mugs and glasses into the dishwasher. Once he set the machine going, he arranged a dozen Irish Coffee glasses in a straight line on the bar, preparing for his favorite pastime when orders were slow—tossing sugar cubes into the glasses.

Before he could dig out the sugar from under the counter however, his cell phone rang. The display showed "Lover." Bethany, his estranged wife. Soon to be ex-wife. What caller ID would he use for Bethany once that happened? Ex? If only? Heart's End? Gabe puffed out a breath. Probably he'd use B Andrews.

"Ciao, bella," he said, when he answered the call. He pulled the box of sugar cubes from beneath the counter.

"Hey Gabe." Her warm, mellow voice stirred memories of the grassy clearing in the woods bordering his Alberta ranch, where he would lie beside her as she twined her fingers in his hair and asked about his day. And he would search for an anecdote that would make her throw back her head and laugh. Because, while he loved her voice, he loved her laugh more.

"The lawyer's office called," she said now. "They have the judgment. Should I tell them to mail it to you?"

His heart sank. The picture of the idyllic clearing at his former ranch splintered into shards. His hand tightened around the sugar cube container, the hard edges of the box biting into his flesh. "Uh, yeah. I guess."

No, he couldn't leave things that way. Too much was tied up with Bethany. "Wait, no," he said. "I'll be there tomorrow. Late. Is that okay?"

"Sure," Bethany said. "But it's Stampede week so hotels are going to be tight. Let me set something up with the hotel we use. I'll call back with details. Bye."

Well crap. And the day had started out upbeat.

The shit disturber that hung out in his head told him, "It's not like you didn't know it was coming."

Yeah, yeah. Didn't mean he had to feel great about it.

"And don't forget," Shit Disturber said, "this was all your idea."

Gabe yelled. "Arrrrgh!" He pitched the container of sugar cubes toward the far wall. Smitty exited the kitchen at the same time as the box hit the wall and broke apart. Ducking rapidly, Smitty lost his grip on the orders he was about to deliver to the mountain bikers.

Burgers somersaulted. French fries followed. Gravy and cheese curds splattered across the bar floor. Sugar cubes bounced off the wall, ricocheting toward Gabe, smacking onto tables, and dribbling along the floor.

Smitty turned back toward the kitchen, saying, "I'll put more burgers on the grill."

Harris entered the room from the back hallway and gazed at their new décor: a mix of poutine, beef patties, and sugar cubes. "I take it something happened?"

"Sorry, buddy." Gabe kicked sugar cubes into the corners of the aisle behind the bar. Then he grabbed a wastebasket and came out into the bar proper. "Probably only six dozen or so, won't take long to pick them up." He tiptoed past a glop of gravy and cheese. "And I'll get a mop."

Harris touched Gabe's arm and said, "What's going on?"

Gabe shook his head and then sighed. "Call from Bethany. I'm gonna drive to Calgary tomorrow, if that's okay with you. Put the final nail in my coffin, so to speak."

Harris stared at Gabe for a minute with a puzzled expression. Then his face cleared, and he nodded. "Ahhh, the divorce. No problem, I'll manage things here until you get back. Want some help cleaning up?"

"Nah, my mess. My responsibility."

Once he'd corralled all the sugar cubes and helped Smitty

mop the floor, Gabe called his sister Lucy in Eau Claire, Alberta. She always cheered him up when things got horrid. When she answered her cell, he said, "Hey Luce, it's me. I'm driving to Calgary tomorrow. Thought I'd stop in at Eau Claire on the return trip and say hi."

"Sorry," Lucy said. "I'm in Toronto with Paul. I won't be home for the next ten days."

"You're with LeBlanc in Toronto in the middle of summer? You hate Toronto."

"Whatever. I'm here and having fun."

"Well, hell. Give my best to LeBlanc," Gabe said. "Tell him the entire region has been enjoying one big party since he left. We're running amok. The place will be in ruins by the time he returns."

7

Tuesday, July 13, 2010

TIFFANY'S CAFÉ

WHEN GABE'S shift at The Peak was over, it was closing in on dinner time. His stomach rumbled, and he hoped Rhonda would have beef stew as the dinner special. She called it boeuf bourguignon and served it over pappardelle. Gabe didn't care what she called it. All he knew, it was beef stew and noodles. It was about the best thing he'd eaten in his life.

It was fast becoming his comfort food. Something that took the sharp edges off the day. After the call from Bethany, it was what he needed right about now.

He slid into his favorite booth and checked out the chalkboard for specials.

Meatloaf.

That did not bode well. The last time meatloaf had been the special Rhonda and her husband had been feuding over who would tell their sixteen-year-old daughter Roxanne she could not get a tattoo. Not on any part of her body, no matter whether it was visible to the public. Rhonda felt Frank should be the one to tell Roxanne because his job as a long-distance trucker kept him away from home for long periods of time, which meant he wouldn't have to face the wrath of Roxanne for more than one or two days a month. Frank wanted

Rhonda to be the heavy because he was a chicken. Everyone who frequented the café knew about the feud, knew the positions of both Rhonda and Frank. The only person, it seemed, who didn't know how Rhonda and Frank felt about tattoos was Roxanne.

The spat had lasted six days. Six days of meatloaf and finally, on a Saturday evening, the regular diners took matters into their own hands and broke the news to Roxanne. "Kiddo," local realtor Cheryl McMillan said, "you can't get a tattoo. Your parents don't want that and trust me, when you get to be my age, you won't want that either. We hate to be the ones to tell you, but Rhonda and Frank are feuding over who should tell you, and meanwhile, we are forced to eat meatloaf. Not that it isn't good meatloaf. But six days now we've had it and no break in sight. We are tired of meatloaf. We want a change. So, there it is. No tattoo. Live with it."

Roxanne merely laughed at Cheryl's comments. "I already decided not to do the permanent tattoo thing. Last Tuesday, Jack's mom showed me a sample of fake tattoos she's thinking of bringing in for the summer fair. You just press them on, and they last about a week. I like that you can change your tattoo."

Tiffany's customers were of two minds: glad the days of meatloaf would come to an end; and frustrated that the feud could have ended four days earlier.

Now here it was again. Meatloaf.

Gabe poured himself a mug of Prince of Darkness coffee while he wondered what the Zaleskos were arguing about now. He returned to his booth just as Rhonda came out of the kitchen, looking frazzled.

She approached his booth. "Want the special?"

"Nuh-uh. How about a burger and fries? And a spinach salad to start?"

She gawked at him. "A salad? You hate salads. You always have the special. What's going on?"

"Can't a guy change it up now and then? I'm worried I'm getting stuck in my ways. Besides, it's meatloaf."

She put her hands on her hips and glared at him. "My meatloaf is the best in the province. You said so yourself. I grind the meat myself, the seasonings are fresh, it's a work of art."

"Yeah, but Rhonda, I ate it six days straight a couple of months ago, and that's pretty much enough for a while. Maybe I'll have it again in about a year."

"Fine. Be like that. Burger and salad. Coming up." She spun on her heel.

"Rhonda, hang on," Gabe said. When she turned to face him again, he said, "Is everything okay at home? You and Frank doing well? Kids okay?"

"Everything is hunky-dory. Why wouldn't it be? Frank's on the road, per usual. The kids are supposed to be here helping but are off gallivanting with their friends, per usual. I'm here and grease is staining my clothes and seeping into my pores and hair. Per usual." She patted her face. "Probably the grease is what's keeping my skin so youthful. I'd love to stay and chat, but I gotta go slap together a salad for a meatloaf hater."

She stomped off to the kitchen.

Gabe traded a "what's up with that?" look with George Finn, who was about to slide into the next booth and had obviously caught Rhonda's parting comments. George was a retired doctor who now owned several businesses in Cheakamus. When George grinned at him, Gabe said, "Hey George, join me. Maybe together we can avoid the minefield that seems to be Rhonda tonight."

"I heard that!" Rhonda said from the kitchen.

George slid into the booth. He leaned forward and said in a low voice, "Apparently Rhonda has this place wired for sound." He sat back, glanced at the menu, and then at the chalkboard. "Hmm, meatloaf. Wonder what's going on in the Zalesko household these days."

"Here's a tip," Gabe said, over the screech of the men's room banshee toilet. "Don't ask."

Rhonda rushed from the kitchen and placed a spinach salad in front of Gabe. It looked slapped together. In fairness, Gabe thought, Rhonda did say she was going to slap a salad together. "This looks great, Rhonda, per usual," he said.

She ignored him and turned to George. "Are you eating tonight, George?"

"Don't I always?" he said. "Let me have your chopped salad, entrée size. I'll help myself to coffee."

"What is it with you guys? I've got enough meatloaf back there to feed the town and most of the surrounding farms."

George rubbed his belly. "I've been eating way too much of your great cooking lately, and now my pants are feeling snug. I must deprive myself for a while. I'm thinking of going on a 'no pie for me' diet. I can't afford to buy a whole new wardrobe."

"Hah!" she said. "You own a men's clothing store. You can get it at cost. Of course you can afford a new wardrobe."

He shrugged and smiled at her. She blew out an exasperated breath. "Fine. Chopped salad for another meatloaf hater. The things you learn about people you thought you knew."

While George busied himself at the rack of coffee thermoses, Gabe slipped into the men's room, retrieved his "out of order" sign from beneath the counter, and stuck it to the door of the banshee toilet.

Gabe was halfway through his spinach salad when Wally Mitchell entered the café and scanned the tables of diners. Gabe waved and slid over to make room. "Be right there," Wally said, before approaching the counter.

Rhonda greeted Wally from the kitchen. "How are things, Wally?"

"Excellent. Even better now that I see what the special is. I'll have meatloaf, extra gravy? And pie for dessert. Whatever you choose for me is fine. I'm sure it will be superb."

When Wally joined them in the booth, Gabe said, "Way to go Wally, make George and me look bad."

"What?"

"Meatloaf," George said.

"You don't like it?" Wally said. "Rhonda's is to die for."

"Weren't you here two months ago when it was the special six days in a row?" Gabe said. "We all sorta overdosed on it."

Wally shook his head. "Guess not."

Rhonda pushed a trolley bearing their entrées to their booth. "Burger and fries." She shoved Gabe's meal down the table to him.

"Chopped salad." She slammed the plate in front of George.

"Special du jour." She gently placed a large plate on the table in front of Wally and turned it so the meatloaf and potatoes were at ten and two, and a mound of succulent looking carrots and Frenched green beans anchored the bottom of the display. "Extra gravy." She placed a gravy boat next to Wally's plate.

Rhonda touched Wally's shoulder. "So nice to serve someone with a discerning palate. For your dessert, I have maple sugar pie and whipped cream."

Gabe's mouth watered. That pie ranked right up there with her beef stew. "Fabulous. I'll have a slice of maple sugar pie, too."

George nodded. "Me too, Rhonda, extra whipped cream."

Rhonda had turned toward the kitchen. She didn't even break stride. "Sorry, I'm all out of pie. And George, you're on a diet. Remember?"

Wally smirked at the others. "Bon appétit," he said.

"Wanna share your pie?" Gabe said.

"Nuh-uh." He lowered his voice. "Word to the wise? *Always* order the special. It hurts her feelings if you don't. And when her feelings are hurt, you don't get pie."

8

Tuesday, July 13, 2010
TIFFANY'S CAFÉ

THEY ATE in silence for a bit. Even when Rhonda was miffed, her food was delicious and Gabe focused on his burger, marveling at whatever secret sauce it was Rhonda spread on the bun. He was positive she laced it with something illegal.

Wally paused while pouring extra gravy onto his meatloaf. "I'm thinking of changing jobs, so I don't have to commute so far every day."

"Got any leads?" George Finn asked.

"No. It's hard to find the ideal job, which for me would be a place where I could spend the day talking books with people."

Gabe said, "Good luck with that. Are you working at the casino tonight?"

"No," Wally said. "I was supposed to work the morning shift, but because of the accident, they shut down the casino until mid-afternoon to give the authorities time to assess things."

"What accident?" Gabe said.

"Wilfred Stillwater. They found him first thing this morning, unconscious in the parking lot. Last I heard, he was in hospital in Silverton. Head injury of some sort. He's in a coma."

"Stillwater," Gabe said. "That name's familiar. Do I know him?"

"Probably not Wilfred," Wally said, "because I don't think he ever comes into Cheakamus. He prefers to stick close to Lake Silverton. But you might know his son, Theo. He partnered with Nestor out at Solomon's Choice Ranch after you and the cops bust the smuggling ring there. Remember, they bought the ranch from the bankruptcy trustee?"

"Oh right, that's where I know the name from."

"What happened in the accident?" George said.

"No one seems to know," Wally said. "Looks like it happened after closing time. No witnesses and the casino cameras didn't catch it. It's weird though. They found his truck butted up against the trees at the edge of the lot, out of gas, transmission in drive."

"Whaaaaat?"

"According to the security guys, the truck's tailgate was down, so they think Wilfred was in the truck's bed. Maybe standing up, moving around, who knows? And somehow the truck must have slipped into drive, knocking him off balance. The speculation is he fell out and hit his head, and the truck moseyed on to the trees."

"Did the Mounties send out their accident reconstruction guys?" Gabe asked.

"Yeah, and hauled his truck off, too."

Rhonda collected their used dishes and placed Wally's maple sugar pie on the table. George and Gabe stared at it and then turned their gazes to Rhonda. "I told ya," she said. "That's the last slice." She looked at Wally. "I overheard you mention Stillwater. Theo? Is he okay?"

Wally shook his head. "Not Theo, his father." He summarized what he knew about the accident and when he mentioned Wilfred was in a coma, Rhonda looked at George Finn.

"What do you think George, will he recover?"

George shrugged. "Back when I practiced medicine, they didn't have as many protocols for treating head injuries. Now, there are a ton of tests they can run and if necessary, they can lessen any pressure on the brain. So I guess the answer is 'it depends.' On Wilfred's general health, his strength, and where exactly his head was traumatized."

"Cripes, I hope he comes out of it. Theo lost his mother a few years ago, and he's an only child, so his father's all he has left."

At the sound of laughter from the front of the café, Gabe looked toward the door and spotted David and Roxanne removing their jean jackets as they maneuvered through the tables toward their mother.

"About time you two showed up," Rhonda said. She tapped the watch on her wrist. "Didn't I ask you to be here before the rush started? Eh? 'Six o'clock,' I said. Where have you been? I've been running off my feet trying to wait on tables, make the food, and do the dishes."

David and Roxanne traded looks.

"And don't do that, either," Rhonda said. "Make faces like I'm nuts. It's a simple thing I asked you to do. Show up on time to help your mother with the dinner rush."

"Roxy's gymnastics practice ran long," David said. "We're only a few minutes late. It's like seven minutes after six." He looked around the café. "And I don't see a rush."

"Well, no thanks to you, there's no rush. You're just lucky that tonight things are slower. When I say six, I mean six."

David and Roxanne slunk away to the back hallway. When Rhonda threw an angry glance at the three men sitting in the booth, George and Gabe ducked their heads and Wally shoveled a forkful of pie into his mouth. "I'll bring your bills," Rhonda said.

"Hoo boy," Gabe whispered. "I think meatloaf's gonna be the special for the next few days. What's got Rhonda all riled up?"

"I don't know," Wally said. "But word to the wise?"

"Yeah, I know," Gabe said. "Order the special."

Gabe said goodnight to the others and made his way to the front to pay for his meal. He glanced at the display of pies Rhonda kept in a case behind the counter. He would know Rhonda's maple sugar pie anywhere and was positive that half of one sat there on the top shelf. He turned toward the cash station where Rhonda waited and saw her watching him. Gabe raised his eyebrows and pointed at the display case.

"Spoken for," she said. "By people who like my cooking."

"Rhonda, I love your cooking. I've loved it since the first morning I discovered this place. I just felt like a burger tonight. It won't happen again, I promise."

Her face crumpled and tears splotched on the countertop. Oh geez, tears. Something Gabe was hopeless at handling. He put a hand on her shoulder, massaging it. "What's going on?"

She sucked in a breath and pulled a tissue from her pocket. After blowing her nose, she said, "Nothing's going on. I'm just tired, I guess. I'm too old for this."

"What do you mean, this?"

She waved at the café. "This. Work. Life. I'm too old."

"Geez," Gabe said. "You're not old, you can't be over..." Luckily, his self-preservation instinct kicked in. "Listen, are you going to be here in the morning? I'm heading out of town and I want to stock up on some of your muffins for the trip."

She nodded and sniffed. "I'll be here. Per usual."

"Great, because I can't leave town without your muffins. You get a good night's sleep, Rhonda. Everything will be better tomorrow." He squeezed her shoulder and left the café.

As he drove the short distance up Lookout Road to the guesthouse and his apartment above the garage in the back alley, Gabe had a brief conversation with the Head Honcho.

"Listen," he said, "I don't have a clue what's going on with my good friend Rhonda, but I imagine you know exactly what's what. She means a lot to me and it would be great if you could sorta take her in hand and help her through whatever it is. I gotta go on a trip, but I'll be thinking about her and checking in with you now and then. I'll try to stay out of trouble so you can focus on Rhonda. Okay? Thanks."

9

Wednesday, July 14, 2010
TIFFANY'S CAFÉ

RHONDA HAD JUST SET the oven timer for an hour when Etta Clayton and her brother Nestor entered the café, loaded down with trays of muffins. "Perfect timing!" Rhonda said as she rushed to meet them.

"We brought extra eggs as well, just in case." Nestor said. "I'll put them in your cooler." When he headed to the kitchen. Etta and Rhonda placed the muffins in the display case. Rhonda's mouth watered as she breathed in the comforting aromas of nutmeg and cinnamon. "Mmmm, I could eat all of them," she said.

"Mango-coconut, peach, and blueberry today," Etta said. "As well as the standby bran and everything-plus-the-sink."

Rhonda wiped her hands and smiled at Etta. They were about the same age, she figured. "How do you manage it all, Etta?" she said. "The ranch, catering, supplying Tiffany's with its goodies? Do you never sleep?"

Etta laughed. "That's one way to do it. You can get a lot done if you don't mess up your days by sleeping. But it seriously messes with your life. Truth is, I hired some help. It was much easier when all I did was cook for the ranch crew and run my little catering business on the side. Not as rewarding, but easier. When we bought the ranch from the trustee, I knew I couldn't do all the cooking we'd need and that Nestor and Theo would be completely hopeless in the kitchen. So I hired people."

"I don't think I can afford to hire anyone else," Rhonda said.

"Well, you don't have to. You have Roxanne and David helping you. And Owen, your new server."

Rhonda nodded. "Owen's okay, so far as it goes. But he doesn't want the early morning shifts. So he does afternoons and some evenings. But my kids, two more years and they will both be off to college or who knows where."

"That's a worry for the future, I think," Etta said.

"Hah, I wish I had your ability to prioritize. I prefer to just dump all my worries into my head at once. Saves time sorting them."

The door blew open and Maxine Lanning came in, lugging a stack of today's edition of *The Journal*. "I can smell those muffins half a block away. What are the choices today?"

When Rhonda listed them for her, Maxine said, "Mango-coconut? I'll take two. Gimme, gimme, gimme!" She placed the stack of newspapers on the shelf beside the door while Rhonda bagged her muffins.

Maxine said. "What's happening with you two?"

Rhonda flashed a wry grin. "I was grousing to Etta about where to find staff these days. Even though, theoretically, I have built-in helpers at home." She leaned against the counter and shrugged. "In seriousness, I'm not sure I'll have my kids as staff much longer. David and Roxy would rather spend time with their friends than slog it out here. When they were fifteen, they thought it was cool that they had an actual job in a café. But the older they get, the harder they are to convince they should work here."

"Here's a thought," Maxine said. "Agree they don't need to work here. See how long they can go without a bit of a salary."

"I don't know. They could find other jobs that pay more."

"Uh-huh," Maxine said. "Let's see how long they take to find other work that offers them all the food they can eat while on the job."

Maxine pulled a piece of muffin from the bag. Rhonda watched her pop the bite into her mouth and chew with her eyes closed. "You look just like him."

"Who?" Maxine said.

"Gabe. The way you close your eyes when you take the first bite of Etta's muffins. Except his favorite is peach. Not saying he would turn down another type if there weren't any peach muffins, but his day might be slightly less perfect."

Maxine said, "I was over at the bar yesterday trying to get the inside scoop on the trouble Gabe got into in Calgary. I found a bunch of stuff in Jacobson's archives and think there might be a story in it. All I got from him was something to do with his ex-wife. And he said it was all off the record. What's up with him?"

"Gabe?" Rhonda said.

"Yes." Maxine's face flushed.

"Asking for a friend?" Rhonda said.

Maxine peered into her paper sack. "Well, you know, he's..." She dug out another piece of muffin and popped it into her mouth. Closed her eyes and chewed. "Mmmm, delicious."

Etta said, "Which one, the muffin or Gabe?"

Maxine raised her eyebrows and smiled. She opened her mouth to speak but closed it as Nestor hurried past them. "Etta, I'll wait outside until you ladies are done with...whatever it is. Not that I overheard anything."

The door slammed behind Nestor, and the women burst

into laughter. "We've shattered his assumptions of what women talk about," Etta said.

Rhonda studied Maxine. Her face was slightly flushed, as if she had a fever. Was it a Gabe-fever? She could have warned Maxine that his heart seemed to hold space for only Bethany. But what the hell, Maxine was a grown woman and sometimes a woman had to find things out for herself.

10

Wednesday, July 14, 2010
TIFFANY'S CAFÉ

BEFORE HE LEFT for Tiffany's on Wednesday morning, Gabe called his landlady, Greta, and told her about the interaction he'd had with Rhonda the previous evening. "Something's bothering her," he said. "She has meatloaf as the special."

"What do you think it is?" Greta said

"I dunno. When I asked, she said she was merely tired and 'too old for this.' I asked what 'this' was, and she said work and life."

"Hmmm. That doesn't sound like our Rhonda."

"How old is she?"

Greta was silent for a moment. "I'm not sure, but I'd say not more than mid-forties. I remember last year she said they'd been married for twenty years. And I know for a fact she finished school before she got married."

"School, as in high school or college?"

"I don't know. That's why I'm guessing she's forty-five at the most. Why?"

"I like to be armed with information in situations when I might stick my foot in my mouth."

Now, as he pulled into a parking spot near the café, Gabe hoped Rhonda was feeling more like herself.

Tiffany's was jammed with the usual horde of breakfast seekers and caffeine junkies when Gabe pushed his way through the entrance. He ordered an extra-large Americano to go from Roxanne, who was working the espresso machine this morning, and half a dozen muffins from Rhonda. "Just give me a selection," he told her, "so I can be surprised when I stick my hand in the bag."

"Where are you heading?"

He grimaced. "Calgary. The divorce judgment is ready. Not an exciting reason to go, but at least I'll have your muffins to keep my spirits up."

Rhonda nodded. "I'm sorry, Gabe."

Gabe studied Rhonda as she bagged the muffins. Her skin color looked better than it had last night, and her hair shone in the morning sunlight. But she still had bags beneath her eyes and her mouth looked pinched.

She handed over the muffins and rang up the purchase. "Ten dollars," she said.

Gabe pulled out his wallet and then stopped. "Wait a minute, that can't be correct. Did you get the Americano as well?"

"Yep. Ten dollars."

He studied the price list above the espresso machine and did the math. "It should be closer to twenty," he said.

"Yeah, and I should have let you have some pie last night. But I didn't because I was being pissy. Ten dollars will ease my conscience."

Rhonda smiled a tired smile. She pushed some errant strands of hair away from her face. "How old do you think I am, Gabe?" she said.

Gabe's stomach clenched. It was a no-win question. "Ahh, well, I have the advantage of knowing some things about you. Like you have kids in high school. I'd say, unless you got married as an underage child, you're in the neighborhood of thirty-seven or thirty-eight. About my age. Another one of us cool thirty-somethings."

"Okay. But how old do I look?"

He had this one. He knew exactly the right answer. "Not a day over thirty."

"Liar."

He held up his hands. "What? I'm not lying. God's truth. Thirty. Okay, maybe thirty-one."

Rhonda sighed. "You're hopeless."

Gabe grinned at her and said, "You take care of yourself. See you in a few days."

As he merged onto the highway toward Alberta, Gabe thought about Rhonda's question. Age, that's what was bothering her. That's why the meatloaf.

11

Thursday, July 15, 2010
SILVERTON HOSPITAL, SILVERTON, B.C.

THE HELPER HAD HIT the old guy with the pipe perfectly. Or so he thought. But the old man's cap must have protected his skull. Because Stillwater didn't die like he was supposed to.

And The Helper couldn't hit him again. The entire plan depended on people thinking Stillwater had fallen out of his truck bed when the transmission slipped. And if The Helper had hit the guy again to finish the job, the cops might realize it wasn't a simple accident.

It had been risky enough, just being in the parking lot with the guy. Hoping everyone had left the casino and gone home, waiting for the right time. It took ages to convince the guy to climb into the truck bed. Then he had to wait for Stillwater to turn his back so The Helper could take aim.

And then wouldn't you know, when he did smack Stillwater, the old guy fell against the side of the truck, not onto the pavement. The Helper had to drag him from the truck bed and position him on the asphalt in the lot to make it appear he'd fallen from the truck.

After that, putting the truck into gear and giving it a little push so it traveled across the lot into the trees had been simple. The Helper had been careful not to touch anything in the truck with his bare hands. He figured he was in the clear.

Except.

Except Stillwater was still alive. In the hospital in Silverton. In a coma. That he could wake up from at any minute. And if he woke up, he'd tell them who had been with him in the parking lot. And how The Helper had been hitchhiking and how Stillwater had given him a lift. How they stopped in the casino lot because The Helper needed to piss. How after The Helper's pee-break he noticed something strange in the truck bed and told Stillwater to come look.

How when Stillwater climbed into the bed, he couldn't see a problem, but before he could ask the kid what he was talking about, things went black.

Now The Helper was outside the Silverton Hospital, by the employee entrance, waiting for someone to come out the door so he could slip inside before the door slammed shut. Then he'd find Stillwater's room, go in, and unplug whatever machine was keeping him on this earth.

Karma always rights the wrongs. A person couldn't escape Karma.

12

Thursday, July 15, 2010
TIFFANY'S CAFÉ

RHONDA SWITCHED OFF THE NEON "OPEN" sign and watched the colors fade. She pulled the blinds down over the door and front windows of the café but left the interior lights on. She had fifteen minutes until Cheryl McMillan was scheduled to show up.

On Tuesday evening, Rhonda had hired Cheryl to sell the café business and to search for a commercial tenant for the upper floor of the café building. Selling the business would mean Frank could ease up, stop doing the long-haul jobs. And leasing out both floors of the building would be a welcome monthly income.

She checked the café's black and white tiled floor. Not as many spots and spills as yesterday. She could start mopping the floor. Maybe by the time Cheryl arrived, she would have it finished.

Or she could have a beer and relax.

She studied the floor. Her back spasmed. The floor could wait.

Rhonda opened the walk-in refrigerator and checked the shelves. Two bottles of Sauvignon Blanc rested on the bottom shelf to the left, beneath the vegetables. A growler of a local brewer's draft beer sat on the cooler floor in front of the back shelves. She hoisted the growler and carried it to the kitchen.

She poured a small glass of beer and took a sip. She winced and studied the glass. The color of the draft was correct. She sniffed. Nothing. She tasted again. Winced again and set the glass down. Vinegar was as close as she could come to describing the taste. How long had the growler been sitting in the cooler? At least since Frank left on the long-haul trip two weeks ago.

A knock sounded at the door and when Rhonda turned toward the sound, Cheryl pushed the door open and entered. A gust of wind followed her. "I think a storm's on its way," Cheryl said. "Am I late?"

"Perfect timing. I was going to offer you beer, but it seems to be off. So, tea is about all I can give you."

"Actually, I've just come from The Peak and if I drink anything else, I will float. I'll be fine without."

Rhonda motioned Cheryl to a booth and, after grabbing a glass of water, joined her. "Any bites on the listing?" she asked.

"Four interested parties so far," Cheryl said. "I've sent all of them the video we made of the café and told them you'd like to interview them. A couple of them were surprised that you wanted to do more than check their financial health."

Rhonda snorted. "Tough. I want to make sure the buyer can actually run a diner and that they will keep the character and ambience of the place intact. I didn't spend years making Tiffany's what it is just to see some know-nothing ruin it."

"There's plenty of goodwill in the café, so a buyer would be nuts to make wholesale changes," Cheryl said. "It's a good idea to talk with the prospective buyers, especially when they will lease the space and equipment from you."

"Can you set up video interviews for me?" When Cheryl nodded, Rhonda asked about the search for a tenant for the upper floor. "We can renovate it to suit the tenant. I use it for events, but it's a blank canvas."

"No bites at the moment, but it's early days," Cheryl said.

Rhonda undid the clasp holding her hair in a messy knot, and ran her fingers through the strands, wondering if the grease in the kitchen was hurting or helping her hair. "The sooner I get this taken care of, the better. I don't seem to have the stamina I had when I was twenty-five. This aging thing is for the birds."

Cheryl said, "I know. Take shoes, for instance." She lifted one leg and waggled her foot, which was clad in a low-heeled espadrille. "I used to wear heels all the time. At least three-inch ones. With pointy toes. Marched all over town in them, showed a gazillion homes to fussy buyers. Not an issue. When I was twenty-five. Now? Not so much."

"Let me ask you something," Rhonda said. "Are you… Do you…"

"Am I, do I what?" Cheryl said.

"I think I'm getting hot flashes. I'm in a bitchy mood most days. And I always feel like crying."

Cheryl snorted. "Two out of the three for me. Always bitchy, always crying."

"I'm worried it's menopause. I'm forty-two and thought I'd have another ten, fifteen years." Rhonda shifted in her seat and rubbed her lower back. "My back hurts. I'm not sleeping. I heard that menopause can give you insomnia."

"I don't think it makes your back hurt," Cheryl said. "Maybe it's from slaving over a hot grill for hours."

Rhonda leaned forward. She hugged herself and spoke barely above a whisper. "I've been spotting, too. Or maybe it's just a weird period? What if it's cancer?"

"What does your doctor say?"

"I haven't gone to see her yet."

Cheryl raised her right eyebrow and stared at Rhonda.

"Yeah," Rhonda said, "I know, I know. But it's so much more fun using the internet to diagnose myself."

"And it's such a great way to give yourself panic attacks,"

Cheryl said. "Those symptoms could be anything. Even pregnancy."

Rhonda raised her hands. "No chance, Cheryl."

"Okay, then. Maybe fibroids? You need to go to your doctor."

"I'm scared to."

"I get that, but fretting about what it could be is bad for your mental health. Get it checked out. It could be nothing."

Rhonda nodded.

She wanted to believe Cheryl. But her gut told her this wasn't nothing.

13

When The Helper Was Seven
ONTARIO

THE BOY WAS in the school playground when he spotted Jeremy and his gang approaching. They were in grade four, two years ahead of him. They were bigger, too.

The boy turned and walked toward the school doors.

"Your dad's a criminal," Jeremy shouted. "He's in jail, isn't he?"

That stopped the boy in his tracks. He turned to face Jeremy. "No, he's not. He's on a special job in Europe."

"Nuh-uh. He stole money. Your mom probably steals too." Jeremy laughed and thumbed his nose at the boy before running up the steps into the school.

Later that afternoon, when his mom came home from her job cleaning houses, he told her what Jeremy had said. "Daddy didn't steal, did he?"

Mom shook her head. "You're old enough to know, I guess. People accused your father of stealing, but they were liars. They lied to the police. They lied to the judge. Everyone ganged up on him."

"Why?"

Mom shrugged. "Because they could. Because they were evil. They ruined his life. They ruined our lives."

"Will Daddy come home soon?"

"Maybe in two more years they might let him out. It's called parole. Meanwhile, we have to live in this dump, and I have to work two jobs. It's all their fault."

Then she smiled and pointed her finger at him. "But karma will get back at them all."

14

Friday, July 16, 2010
TIFFANY'S CAFÉ

RHONDA PUSHED her fringe off her face with the back of her hand and surveyed Tiffany's Café. The front windows were steamy, partly from the warmth of the café and partly from the rainstorm raging outside. Cheryl McMillan's prediction last night of a coming storm had been correct. Friday started out with threats of rain and progressed to a full-on summer squall, intent on dumping a month's worth of rain in hours.

Most of the townspeople evidently decided to wait out the weather at the café. Every table and booth was occupied; two stools remained open at the counter. The clack of the espresso dispenser punctuated the conversations and laughter that swirled through the diner. Owen sprinted among the tables to keep up with requests from hungry patrons.

Order slips danced on the wire clothesline strung across the kitchen opening. Burger patties and bacon sizzled on the grill; fries bubbled in the deep fryer. The lunch rush was as fierce as the storm outside.

Rhonda plated a lemongrass chicken salad and dinged the bell. "Day three of George's healthy lunches," she called out. When Owen collected the order and delivered it to George

Finn, applause began. Slowly at first, building to a standing ovation. George grinned and bowed to the crowd.

Rhonda pointed toward the wall by the café entrance, and the dry erase calendar with the heading "When will Doc Finn Order Pie?" Several of the calendar days were filled in with names and comments. "The pot's rising," Rhonda said. "Fifty-eight dollars at last count. Only a toonie to play."

Last Tuesday, George had announced he was going on a diet. "No more of Rhonda's pie," he'd said. "No more fun for me." He professed the diet was because his clothes felt tight. But Rhonda knew his statement was a sly way to avoid ordering the meatloaf special she'd had on the menu that evening.

Ever since then, Rhonda had called George's bluff. She added "Daily Dietary Special" to her chalkboard menu, knowing that George would feel obliged to order it. Then she set up a pool for townspeople to become invested in George's progress, inviting them to guess when George would finally cave in and order pie.

"What are the odds?" a voice asked.

"Way better than the odds on the pool over at The Peak Bar," Rhonda said. "At least this one might be winnable, because we all know George can't resist my apple pie. Or any pie, for that matter."

George spoke up. "True. But I'm all about willpower. And the pool at The Peak depends on Gabe's skill tossing sugar cubes into Irish Coffee glasses. Eventually, he has to miss."

"He hasn't missed yet, and it's been almost seven months," Rhonda said. "What's the pot at now? Four thousand?"

Shortly after the rush died down and the café began to empty, Maxine Lanning entered, shook the raindrops from her raincoat, and slid onto a stool at the far end of the counter, well away from the remaining diners. Rhonda placed cutlery on the counter in front of her. "Hey, Max, you're running late today. Lucky for you, I have one order of the lemongrass chicken salad left."

"Yum, lemme have it."

When Rhonda delivered the salad, Maxine said, "I was at Silverton Lake this morning on a story. At one point, I worried I wouldn't even get back to town in time for dinner, never mind lunch. And not just because of the storm."

"Anything you can talk about?" Rhonda asked.

Maxine glanced around the café and then lowered her voice. "Yeah, but keep it under wraps until I get the story into the paper. There was a sailing accident at the lake. A woman fell overboard and died. A tourist, not a local. I have almost no details, despite being out there all morning."

Maxine speared a piece of lemongrass chicken. Chewed, swallowed, and groaned. "Oh man, this is a party in my mouth." She glanced at Rhonda and shook her head. "No life jacket. Who goes out on the water alone without one? Especially in weather like this."

Rhonda said, "Because we are all immortal. At least, before we hit middle age." Gawd, was she middle-aged? Is that what was going on with her body—age? If so, it was pretty damn unfair to get hit with menopause before even one gray hair had sprouted. Maybe she should go to the doctor. Yeah, no. Why run the risk that a professional would confirm her youth was over?

As she headed back to the grill, Rhonda's phone pinged, signaling an incoming text. She tapped the screen. Beneath an unknown number and the flag "possibly spam" appeared a brief text message: "Karma is waiting. U R next."

Bloody hell. No doubt the next text would ask for money. Canada needed better regulations for communications. All the Russian bots were overrunning the system.

15

When The Helper Was Nine
ONTARIO

On a breezy summer morning, the boy sat on the swing in the schoolyard across the street from his house. He scuffed the toes of his sneakers in the dust as he idly moved back and forth. Mom had sent him outside to play because she wanted to vacuum and didn't need him underfoot.

But he knew the truth.

Mom wasn't going to vacuum. She wanted her morning drink. She thought he didn't know. She thought he believed the vodka in her glass was plain water. But he'd tasted it once when she wasn't looking. Yuk. It burned his throat. How could she like that stuff?

All the other kids were away at camp. Mom said they had no money for him to go. Maybe if she didn't spend all her money on vodka, he could have gone to camp. Summer holidays sucked. Except this one, maybe. Because Mom said Dad was coming home soon. His parole hearing was only a week away and then she was sure he'd be let out of prison and would join them here. He'd get a good job, and they would be a family again and everything would be wonderful. His stomach tingled when he thought about having a dad again.

A gray car came along the street and stopped in front of his house. A brown-haired woman got out and walked to their front door. Miss Monroe. The social worker who always smiled at him and ruffled his hair. He liked her. Mom said Miss Monroe was spying on them, trying to cut them off. "She's just like all the rest," Mom said. "Waiting for a chance to screw us over."

He leaped from the swing, ran across the street, and went inside his house. Mom and Miss Monroe were in the small kitchen, sitting at the table. "Legionnaire's Disease," Miss Monroe said. "I'm so sorry, Louise."

Mom slammed her glass down, splashing the contents onto the tabletop. "Sorry? You're sorry? What the hell good is that going to do me, that you're sorry? He never should have been in that prison to start with."

"Mom? What's happened?"

Mom's face was flushed. She wiped a tear from her eye. "Daddy's dead. He's not coming home. You and I are all alone now."

The boy sobbed. "I don't want him to be dead."

Mom shouted, "Well, he is! And it's all because of those people in Cheakamus."

Miss Monroe sighed. "Louise, you know that's not true. Al embezzled money. That's why he was in prison."

Mom turned on Miss Monroe. "What the hell do you know? You weren't there. I was. The fink accountant at Al's company set him up. I bet he's enjoying the money himself. And then we had to use a free lawyer. Legal aid, they call it. Hah! Some aid he gave Al. The guy couldn't defend a traffic ticket, never mind embezzlement. And the prosecutor and judge were against Al from the start. The jury too. I mean, most of them were from the town. Unbelievable that they would turn on one of their own."

Mom stopped and took a breath. Then she smiled. "But

karma will even things up. They'll all learn what it's like to lose someone unfairly. I hope they all suffer the way we've suffered."

16

Friday, July 16, 2010
EAU CLAIRE, ALBERTA

FRIDAY MORNING, a few hours after the sun finally peeked over the eastern horizon, Gabe left Calgary and headed west in Three, his black F150. In fact, the truck was Gabe's third black F150 in as many years. The first two had met untimely ends: one planted its nose into a haystack when Gabe decided to drive cross country in the dark. The other dove off a pier at Eau Claire Lake when Gabe's foot found the gas pedal instead of the brake.

Gabe enjoyed discussing the day and life in general with his trucks. Invariably they listened and rarely spoke out of turn. Even though he thought of his truck as a "he," Gabe had opted for a neutral name. Three.

Now he said, "You probably wanted to hang around Calgary, eh Three? But we both know it's not always chuckwagon breakfasts, street dancing, and hay bale décor. The Stampede only lasts for ten days and then we'd be back in reality. So, here's the plan. We're heading to Canmore for coffee and a muffin, and then we're going home."

He'd had an excellent Americano and croissant at Le Germain before checking out, but more fuel was called for. He rubbed his eyes.

Gabe hadn't really slept after Beth left in the wee hours. A thunderstorm had moved through the city, and he'd stood at the window watching the lightning flash across the sky. And remembering their night. Remembering all their other nights. And wishing there could be more.

The document he and Bethany had received from their lawyer sat on the passenger seat, an unwanted but necessary companion. The words "Divorce Judgment" were small but packed an immense weight. Fifteen letters, when put together in that order, spelled a formal end to his marriage. The judgment would be effective in thirty-one days. The time lapse was intended to give the spouses time to rethink the situation, to appeal the judgment.

Neither he nor Bethany would do that. This was the plan he had put in motion last October when Bethany's job at the network was jeopardized because she was married to an accused murderer. It didn't matter that Gabe wasn't guilty of murder. Nor did it matter that the charges were dropped. People in Calgary still remembered that the husband of Bethany Andrews, local television news host and reporter, had been arrested on suspicion of murder. And that was what they would continue to remember until the person who killed Andover Drake was found and convicted.

Gabe snorted. Like that would happen. The Calgary cops had written Drake's murder off as another one for the cold case files and had moved on to other cases. Which meant no one except Gabe was looking into it anymore. And he was getting nowhere with his investigation.

So, Gabe had told Bethany to divorce him. That way, she would be seen as a woman who took charge of her life and cast bad things from it. And it worked. Her job was safe. She had a new image around the city. Bethany Andrews, the woman who shook off an unfortunate spouse.

He glanced at the Divorce Judgment sitting on the seat. He supposed he should be thankful they didn't have children.

Less messy to dissolve a relationship when there were only two people involved. No small ones wondering what they had done to make mommy and daddy separate. No littles thinking they had to choose sides.

But also, no lives to carry the Andrews-Gabrieli bloodstream into the future, something Gabe had always believed would happen. But Bethany needed to focus on solidifying her position at the network. "I can't afford to take a mat leave," she had said every time the subject came up. "The viewers will forget me, and eager interns are just waiting for the chance to sit in the anchor chair."

"How about I take a leave for a year instead?" Gabe had asked. "Or take the baby to the office with me?"

Bethany had laughed off the suggestion. "Let's wait a bit, for the right time," she said.

Before the right time came along, Drake got himself killed, Gabe got himself arrested, and everything went to rat shit.

He grabbed the document and stuffed it into the center console. When he got to Cheakamus, he'd file it away with the other mementos of his once happy marriage. Would he mark the thirty-one days on his calendar so he knew when his marriage was officially done? Not a chance. Would he still be aware of the clock ticking down? Absolutely.

The road sign announcing a junction with Highway 22 caught Gabe's eye. Eau Claire, his hometown and the place where both his mother and his sister Lucy still lived, was perhaps half an hour away. Since Lucy was in Toronto with LeBlanc, Gabe had abandoned the idea of going to Eau Claire. But now he realized Mercy, his mother, would be at home in Eau Claire.

"Hold on, Three. Change of plans."

He turned left at the junction. It would be good to see his mother. Take her to Wright's Café for breakfast. Fill her in on the news from his life.

Half an hour later, when Gabe pulled to a stop outside

Mercy's house, he spotted her hauling the garbage bin to the curb. She wore a dark red skirt that swirled around her calves, a black, lacy pullover sweater, and a full-length vest that rivaled a gypsy tapestry in its mix of colors and textures. That was Mercy—bohemian to the core.

When she noticed his truck, she waved and waited for him to join her on the sidewalk. "Sunny! What a surprise! Why didn't you tell me you were in town?"

"Hey Mom." Gabe bent down and kissed Mercy on her cheek. "I was in Calgary on business and thought I could take you to Wright's Café before I get back on the road to Cheakamus."

"I have coffee on here if you like?"

"Mom. The famous cinnamon rolls at Wright's Café? How often do I get to enjoy one? Especially with you?"

They scored the last table for two at the café. Better yet, the young server at the counter told Gabe they had not yet sold out of cinnamon rolls. "Let me have two rolls and two coffees for here," he said. He took a step toward the table where Mercy had settled and then turned back to the server. "And two more rolls to go. I've got a long drive ahead."

Minutes after Gabe joined Mercy at the table, she glanced across the room when the door opened, and waved. "Jennifer, hi!"

Mercy tapped Gabe's arm. "Look, it's Jennifer Sugar. You remember her, right?"

Gabe glanced toward the doorway and, in addition to spotting Jennifer, noticed her vintage blue and white Volkswagen van angle-parked directly outside the café.

"Looks like she's still driving her ode to the seventies," he said. "And she's obviously still a cop."

Jennifer's uniform was crisp and clean, her long, streaky blond hair was knotted neatly at the base of her neck, and the handcuffs on her belt glinted under the café's lighting. She turned then and waved at him, a playful grin appearing on her face.

Jennifer clutched her coffee and approached their table. Gabe rose slightly from his seat. "Hey, Jen. Want to join us?"

She shook her head. "Another time, perhaps. Just wanted to say hi."

"Any news about the new police chief?" Mercy asked Jennifer.

"There's a new chief in the department?" Gabe asked.

Jennifer sipped her coffee. "No news other than I heard interviews are almost done and there are at least two top candidates." Then she addressed Gabe. "Our current chief is retiring soon."

Gabe was tempted to ask if Jennifer was one of the two contenders. She was intuitive and analytical, two qualities that made for excellent detectives. He opened his mouth, but Jennifer changed the subject.

"Still living in Cheakamus, Gabe? Don't the mountains make you feel trapped?"

"You mean the fact that you can't see the horizon unless you climb one of them? Or the fact that the sun is late to rise above the peaks, and early to sink below them?"

Mercy jumped in. "I'm in Cheakamus often. You get used to it. And I always feel like the mountains are protecting me, embracing me."

Gabe snorted. "No, a person doesn't get used to it. The sky is smaller there. But even so, Cheakamus has a way of burrowing its way into you. The town and the residents. So, yeah, I'm still living there."

Jennifer studied Gabe for a beat and then checked her watch. "Oops, gotta run. Nice chatting with you both." With a wave, she spun on her heel and hurried to the exit.

Gabe hadn't learned if Jennifer was in the running for the Chief's job. But Mercy would know—his mother was a lot like his landlady Greta Rocque: the roots of the town's grapevine.

He said, "Is Jennifer…" and was interrupted by the ringing of his mother's cell phone.

She raised a finger at him. "Hang tight."

17

Friday, July 16, 2010
TIFFANY'S CAFÉ

THE MID-AFTERNOON RUSH ended about the same time as the storm blew its last gust. Now the sun blazed down on the wet streets, making them sparkle.

Rhonda had finished checking the cash for the day's bank deposit when Maxine rushed into the café, slid onto a counter stool, and said, "Update! Update! Hear all about it!"

Rhonda slammed the cash drawer closed, poured herself a mug of coffee, and plunked herself onto a stool beside Maxine. "I'm in luck," Rhonda said. "The café's empty for a change and I have nothing on my to-do list but listen to the news you are about to drop into my ears."

"Absolutely right," Maxine said. "I was out at Silverton Lake again and found out more information about the sailing accident. You'll never guess who the victim is."

Rhonda waited, and when Maxine didn't continue after a few seconds, said, "Well?"

"I thought you'd guess."

"Max, if you say I'll never guess who it is, why would I try? So, tell me."

"Lara Quinn."

"Who?"

"The judge's sister. Lara Quinn. Kathaleen's older sister visiting from Vancouver."

Rhonda's jaw dropped. "Omigod! Does Kathaleen know?"

Maxine jumped up, hurried to the coffee thermoses, and poured a mug of Prince of Darkness before returning to the counter stool. On the return trip, she said, "Yes, of course. As soon as the police found out from the rental shop at the lake who had rented that sailboat, they called Judge Quinn. She immediately adjourned court for the day and drove from Trail to the lake, where she identified Lara."

"She must be heartbroken."

"Definitely, she was crying," Maxine said. "But after a few minutes, she spoke with the police constable at the site and then became visibly angry. So much so that the cop started backing away from her, hands up as if to say, 'don't hurt me.'"

"What did she say to the cop?"

Maxine shrugged. "Wish I knew. I stopped her as she started to leave the site and asked if I could interview her about her sister. She shot me a look that told me 'over my dead body' and stomped off."

Rhonda nodded. "She's ferocious when aggravated. Years ago, I had jury duty, and she was the judge. She was newly appointed, and I think the defense lawyer figured he'd be able to walk all over her. Hoo-boy, was he wrong."

"What happened?"

"He kept interrupting the prosecutor with objections, which I gathered weren't solid because Judge Quinn continually overruled him. Once she even said, 'Counsel, a first-year law student knows that pig won't fly.' Finally, after the umpteenth objection, she said she wanted to see both lawyers in chambers. Then she smiled serenely at the jury and asked us to excuse her for a moment."

Rhonda sipped her coffee and grinned. "I don't know what she said to the lawyers during that meeting, but five minutes later, when they all came back into the courtroom, the prosecutor was working hard not to grin. And the defense lawyer was white in the face. His hands visibly shook when he picked up his pen at his table."

"Ahh, the police constable's reaction to her at the lake makes sense," Maxine said.

"Yeah, don't mess with Judge Quinn."

"I've never had jury duty," Maxine said. "How was it?"

Rhonda shrugged. "Not bad. Worst part was when they sequestered us, I couldn't tend to the café. Frank had to handle it. And the kids were young, so he had to manage them too." Then Rhonda chuckled. "Actually, that might have been the best part, because both he and the kids realized what it was like to get along without me."

Of course, Rhonda knew, it had also made her recognize how dear her family was to her.

18

When The Helper Was Eleven
ONTARIO

"C'MON," Mom said. "We're going to Burger Palace. Burgers and fries. Maybe milkshakes too."

The boy's stomach rumbled, and his mouth watered at the thought of a burger from Burger Palace. Juicy patty. Bacon and fried onions. Barbecue sauce dripping down the side. They hardly ever went to the Burger Palace unless it was a special occasion.

And it usually meant that for the next week they lived on mac and cheese. The boxed kind. Mom's welfare money went quickly each month. Rent and her vodka left a small amount for food. The boy cut the neighbors' lawns in the summer and delivered the local newspaper each week, using his earnings to buy fruit and vegetables. He knew better than to keep the cash. Even if he hid it, Mom would hunt it out and use it for booze.

"Why?" he asked.

"Do we need a reason?" Mom said. Then she laughed. A sharp, rapid-fire burst. "How about celebrating life and how great it's been for us?"

It hadn't been a glorious life so far as he could see. But he was hungry and loved burgers. So, he wouldn't refuse the chance. If Mom wanted to celebrate life, he'd go along with it.

After lunch, when they got into the car, Mom said, "Let's go for a drive. What do you say?"

He looked at the gas gauge. "Do we need to stop for gas?"

Mom shook her head. She snapped the top open on her water bottle, chugged, and laughed. Again, that high-pitched burst. It sounded weird. But then his mom didn't laugh often. Or ever. "Nope. There's plenty in the tank for where we're going."

She drove out of town onto the two-lane highway that snaked through the countryside. "I hate this place," Mom said. She sipped from her water bottle. "The only reason we have to live here is because of all those rotten bastards in Cheakamus."

The same refrain he'd heard all his life. He had it memorized. He knew the names of all the people who messed up his dad's life, Mom's life. And his own.

But then Mom said something new. "Well, we don't have to put up with it anymore. We don't have to live a crummy life if we don't want to. Do we?"

Maybe Mom had found a new job. Maybe things were going to change. The car drifted toward the highway's shoulder. The boy gasped. "Watch out, Mom. You're close to the edge."

She cranked the steering wheel to the left, and the car lurched into the oncoming lane.

"Mom!"

"Sorry. My bad." She straightened the car out. "But you're right, son. I am close to the edge. In fact, I'm over it. Why am I busting my ass in this two-bit town? Why do I have to put up with the sneers of the snotty women in town who think they're better than me? Why are we relying on the food bank? Because your dad went to jail, that's why. Because he went to jail and then he died, and things will never change now."

"We could move, Mom. Go somewhere new. Start over."

She guzzled the contents of the water bottle. Some spilled down her chin and onto her blouse. She swiped at it with her free hand and the car swerved toward the ditch. At the last second, she caught the wheel and whipped the car back into the lane. "Start over? With what? We have no money. The last of it went on lunch. There's nothing left—nothing for gas to leave town, nothing to pay for another place to live. Nothing."

She tipped the bottle up and drained it in one gulp. "Ahh. Grey Goose, nothing but the best for my last trip." She pressed on the gas pedal.

"Mom, slow down, okay? You're going too fast."

"It's okay, honey. Life is no fun, is it? But soon everything will be okay. You won't have to worry about a thing anymore."

The road climbed steeply. The boy saw a sharp turn to the left at the top of the hill. The car gained speed. His Mom's eyes were fixed on the road.

"Mom! Slow down. Stop the car. I feel sick. I'm gonna throw up. Let me out, Mom!"

"Soon son. It won't matter anymore."

They reached the top of the hill, and Mom kept the car pointed straight ahead.

"Mom! Nooooo!"

The car smashed through the low metal barrier at the edge of the road, careened over the edge, and crashed into the trees fifty feet below.

19

Friday, July 16, 2010
EAU CLAIRE, ALBERTA

"HELLO, LOVE," Mercy said into her phone. She glanced at Gabe and mouthed, "Seamus."

Seamus O'Malley, owner of the Preferred Stock ranch outside Cheakamus, had been Mercy's significant other for several years. They seemed to be the proof of the adage "absence makes the heart grow fonder." Mercy insisted it was the ability to lead independent lives that kept their relationship alive and beating.

A year ago, Gabe's teenaged brother Jack had moved to Cheakamus to live at the O'Malley ranch. Jack had moved there reluctantly, believing he was being exiled and nicknaming Seamus "the Warden." Gabe had his own issues with Seamus, tolerating the old Irishman only because Mercy adored the guy. However, partly because of a case Gabe had investigated last fall, Jack had matured, Seamus had mellowed, and Gabe grudgingly admitted the rancher was a likeable man.

"What?" Mercy said into the phone. "Hang on, Gabe is with me. I want him to hear this." She tapped the speaker button and placed the phone on the table. "Seamus, tell Gabe."

"I was telling your mother," Seamus said. "Terrible accident at Silverton Lake this morning. A woman out on the lake alone in her sailboat in the middle of a nasty storm. Smacked in the head by the boom and knocked into the water, they say. Drowned, they say."

Gabe sucked in his breath, afraid to hear Seamus's next words.

Then he relaxed. No. If the sailor had been someone close to Gabe, Seamus would have started the discussion with "I'm sorry."

"Who was it?" Gabe asked.

"Dunno. Might have been a tourist."

Mercy said, "People are going to say Cheakamus is jinxed. First, Wilfred Stillwater gets run over by his own truck at the casino! Now this."

"No, Mercy," Seamus said, "his truck didn't run over him. He fell from the truck's bed and hit his head on the asphalt."

"Whatever," Mercy said. "I mean, how bizarre. At least he didn't die like this poor woman in the lake. You know how skittish tourists can be. Any more accidents and they will avoid the town like the plague."

Gabe thought back to the accident involving Stan Wurtz's parents. That made three in the last two months. It was weird that there would suddenly be a cluster of accidents. Unless, as his mother said, the town was jinxed.

Had the Frikkin Comedian expanded his targets to include people in Cheakamus? Gabe shook that thought from his head instantly. Best not to even entertain that idea.

He excused himself to collect his takeout order from the server. When he returned to the table with his bag of cinnamon rolls, Mercy had finished her discussion with Seamus. She said, "Seamus told me to tell you that steer is looking forward to a rematch. Are you playing cowboy again?"

Gabe shrugged.

Mercy lifted her coffee mug to her mouth and studied him as she sipped. "You look tired, Sunny."

Well yeah, his farewell tour with Bethany.

He stretched and yawned. "Didn't get much sleep last night."

"Oh?" Mercy's lifted eyebrows asked the question, "Why?"

Rule number one of sons of mothers everywhere, at least the sons Gabe knew: no matter how old you are, your mother still thinks of you as that kid she walked to school on your first day in grade one. That kid who believed birds and bees were mere beings in the garden.

He said, "Hotel beds. I'll be glad to get back to my own."

She accepted his statement at face value and then asked, "What was the business that took you to Calgary?"

He gave his mother a weak smile. "Bethany and I received the divorce judgment yesterday. It's all wrapped up."

"Oh, sweetheart, I'm sorry." Then his mother's face hardened. "But I'm also not sorry. I never thought Bethany was right for you. You deserve someone who stands by you through thick and thin."

"Mom, don't start."

Mercy raised her hands. "Alright, alright. I'm just saying there are many better women out there."

"If you say so. But I ain't looking."

"I know you aren't. That's the problem."

"Mom."

"Fine," Mercy said. She finished the last bite of her cinnamon roll and wiped her mouth. "Mostly, the trouble is that you're a small-town boy. Instead of falling for big-city Bethany, you should have focused on small town girls. Like Jennifer Sugar. Didn't you date her in high school?"

Gabe really didn't want to talk about his romantic life with his mother. Almost as much as he didn't want to talk about his sex life. But perhaps it would get his mother off the topic of

Bethany. "We had one date at least twenty years ago. No, call it half a date. I was gonna take her canoeing at Eau Claire Lake. Remember how you used to cover the canoe with a blue tarp?"

Mercy nodded. "Yes, to keep the elements out."

"Well, it didn't keep a mother skunk out."

"Oh, no!"

Gabe nodded. "Yeah, Jennifer was standing right in the line of fire when I pulled the tarp away. And mama skunk let loose. Jennifer changed her mind about canoeing then, at least with me."

Mercy giggled. "Sorry. I'm not laughing at you. I'm laughing at the situation."

Gabe drained his coffee and stood. "Ready, Mom?"

When he dropped Mercy back at her house, she said, "I'm sure Jennifer forgave you for the skunk."

Gabe snorted. "Hah. Jennifer Sugar is more about getting even."

20

Saturday, July 17, 2010

TIFFANY'S CAFÉ

GABE SAT in his favorite booth at the back of Tiffany's, working on his third coffee of the day and waiting on his burger and fries. He scrolled through the messages on his phone, looking for an update from Lucy. Was she still in Toronto, living large with LeBlanc? Was she ghosting him? Did she and LeBlanc run off and get married?

Imagine being LeBlanc's brother-in-law. Gabe grinned and shook his head. LeBlanc would have to use Gabe's first name instead of "Gabrieli." The grin fell away. Wait a minute, that meant Gabe would have to call LeBlanc "Paul". Well hell, that would be like meeting the guy all over again.

And their first meeting hadn't been all that hot. LeBlanc had stood at the crime scene, arms folded across his chest, his face a mask of cold superiority that cops adopted to keep normal people out of their lives. "Think it was an accident?" Gabe had asked.

"Too early to tell," LeBlanc said. Next question, same answer. Gabe detected LeBlanc's French accent. Perhaps those were the only English words the cop knew.

Now, six months after that initial chilly reception, Gabe knew better. Paul LeBlanc was as fluent in English as in

French. Gabe knew enough French swear words to recognize when LeBlanc was pissed off—sometimes with a situation, often with Gabe. They had developed a rough, bantering, grudging friendship of sorts.

Well, they'd had to, hadn't they? Lucy had flicked her hair as she sauntered away from LeBlanc one afternoon, and the poor sucker was hooked. And because Lucy was dear to Gabe, and she wanted to spend time with LeBlanc, Gabe accepted the cop as part of his close circle.

Probably, if pushed, Gabe would admit that he liked LeBlanc. Sort of. Maybe. Now and then. He had filed LeBlanc under "Bearable, barely."

Owen placed Gabe's lunch on the table. "Condiments?" he asked.

"Wow, Owen. Another fancy word. Is Rhonda trying to get a Michelin star?"

Owen grinned and shook his head. "Nah. I was doing some reading about chef things and restaurants. Condiments are sauces you can put on your meal."

Gabe grabbed the ketchup bottle from the rack in the booth. He upended it and spurted a thin stream of red deliciousness onto his plate.

"Yep, I know. I can even spell condiment. K E T C H U P. And now and then it's spelled M U S T A R D."

Gabe silenced his phone and dug into the burger. Juicy patty, luscious fried onions, sharp melted cheese, the secret sauce, and a firm slice of beefsteak tomato layered between toasted brioche bun halves. He raised his face upward, closed his eyes, hummed, and silently thanked the Head Honcho for Rhonda and her burgers. And the secret sauce. One of these days, he'd get the secret from her. Until then, he would just keep eating at Tiffany's.

When he opened his eyes, a woman stood beside his booth. He blinked, swallowed, and wiped his mouth with his napkin. "Sorry," the woman said, "didn't mean to startle you."

"Uh huh. No problem."

"You're Gabe Gabrieli, the detective," she said.

"Yep."

She looked to be about Greta's age. Maybe a tad younger. Say fifty-five. Shortish, perhaps five-three. Trim. Dark, short-cropped hair shot with silver. Enormous blue eyes. She clutched a mug of coffee in one hand and fiddled with her pearl earring with the other. Then she chewed her lip, ending up with a touch of red lipstick on her teeth. "Umm, I'm Kathaleen Quinn," she said. "Can I talk to you?"

He hesitated and glanced down at his burger, cooling on the plate.

"It's important. You eat and I'll talk. How's that?"

Gabe waved his hand toward the opposite bench seat. "Have at it." He grabbed up his burger and took another bite, dabbing at the sauce that dribbled beside his mouth.

Quinn sat across from him and sucked in a huge breath. "My sister has been killed. I need you to investigate her murder."

Gabe choked.

"You know I'm a private investigator, right? Not police."

She nodded. "Yes, I checked you out."

"And you also know that the police are the ones to investigate murders, right?"

"They aren't investigating this one. That's why I'm coming to you."

"So, it's a cold case?"

She shook her head and took a sip of coffee. Her eyes teared. She dug through her bag, found a tissue, and wiped her eyes. "No, they say it was an accident. I know better."

Gabe dipped two fries into the puddle of ketchup on his plate and popped them into his mouth. They were cold. He chewed and studied Quinn. Then he waved at Rhonda, who was chatting with a diner sitting at the counter. "Rhonda!"

Rhonda interrupted her conversation and waved at Gabe.

When the young diner at the counter swung around on his stool, Gabe noted suntanned skin and Ray-Bans perched atop shaggy, shoulder-length hair. He filed the fellow under "dude, surfer."

"Got a minute?" Gabe asked Rhonda.

She hurried over, wiping her hands on her apron. "Something wrong with your meal, Gabe?" When she glanced at Quinn, Rhonda said, "Hi Judge. So sorry about your sister."

"Thanks Rhonda," Quinn said. "I'm hoping Mr. Gabrieli will look into the so-called accident for me."

Gabe stared at Quinn.

Judge?

Gabe liked to avoid judges. About as much as he liked to avoid cops and courtrooms. In his experience, nothing much good came out of a courtroom. Case in point #1: an arraignment on a murder charge. Case in point #2: a divorce.

"Gabe? Gabe! What's wrong with your meal?" Rhonda said.

He snapped out of his reverie. "Oh, sorry, I was chatting with Ms., I mean Judge, Quinn here and my fries got kinda cold and neglected. I was hoping I could get a re-do?"

Rhonda grabbed his plate. "Only for you, Gabe. And only because if you're sitting here chatting with the Judge it means you're planning to help her out, right?"

"Dunno yet."

Rhonda straightened her back, glared at him, and said, "Well, let's see." She lifted a finger. "One, my special secret sauce, to which you are addicted, is congealing on your burger." Second finger. "Two, your fries are looking kinda limp." Third finger. "Three, you are hungry. I can toss this in the garbage and give you a new burger and fries. Free. Or you can refuse to help the Judge, and I can let you finish this cold, congealed meal. Which, of course, you will pay full price for."

Gabe shrugged and flashed a grim smile. "You forget I can slip across to The Peak, where we also have burgers and fries.

Or I can go knock on Greta's door and play my 'poor, poor, pitiful me' card and she will feed me."

Rhonda lifted a fourth finger. "Four, I know about the 'out of order' sign you stick on the men's room stall whenever you want to sit in this booth and enjoy a quiet meal."

She smiled at Judge Quinn and said, "There's a toilet in there that howls like a witch when it's flushed, so no one wants to use this booth because the noise ruins their meal. Except for Gabe, here, who slaps an out-of-order sign on that stall ensuring no one uses that toilet while he's eating."

She turned back to Gabe and lifted her thumb. "Five, I'll ban you from any other table but this one and I'll take away your sign."

Gabe lifted his hands in surrender. "Nooooo, not my sign! Okay, here's the deal. Fresh burger and fries, whatever the Judge wants to eat, and a slice of your maple sugar pie. On the house. How's that sound?"

"I suppose you want whipped cream on the pie?"

"Well, duh, Rhonda."

Rhonda turned to Quinn. "What can I get for you?"

"That maple sugar pie sounds about right."

"Whipped cream?"

Quinn grinned. "Well, duh, Rhonda."

When Rhonda headed for the kitchen, Gabe said, "I like to get Rhonda fired up now and then. It makes her feel good to believe she forced me to do something. But in truth, all along I was planning on at least hearing your story to see if I can help."

"Do you really have an 'out of order' sign for the screeching toilet?"

"Yep."

"I admire your creativity." Quinn paused and then said, "Can I tell you about the so-called accident?"

Gabe nodded. When he relaxed against the back of the seat, he exchanged a wave with Smitty, who was collecting takeout. Gabe made a note to remind Smitty that part of his pay at The Peak Bar was free meals. No need for him to take out from Tiffany's. Unless, of course, Smitty was as addicted to Rhonda's secret sauce as Gabe was.

Judge Quinn cleared her throat, and Gabe turned his attention back to her.

"Lara was found in Silverton Lake Friday morning. Drowned. Her sailboat was drifting nearby. The police learned she had rented the boat earlier that day. It was very stormy on the lake, so they speculate the boat's boom swung around and hit her, knocking her into the water. Where she drowned."

"And what bothers you about their theory?"

"Lara was an experienced sailor. I doubt she'd put herself in a spot where the boom could hit her."

Gabe shrugged. "Things happen."

"But most of all," Quinn said, "it's the life vest." When she noticed Rhonda approaching with their orders, Quinn interrupted her story. "Thanks Rhonda, this looks superb."

"Well, duh, Judge. Of course it is," Rhonda said with a sly grin before moving away.

"What about the life vest?" Gabe asked as he squirted ketchup onto his plate.

"She wasn't wearing one." Quinn leaned forward and fixed her eyes on Gabe. Her hands clenched. "I'm telling you, Lara would never have been in that boat without a life vest. Never. She's always been...was... anal about personal safety."

Gabe bit into his burger and savored the spices in Rhonda's secret sauce.

"Okay," he said after he swallowed. "Tell me about Lara." He pushed his plate aside and dug his pen and notebook from his pocket.

"She lived in Vancouver and was here visiting me on a break. She and her husband divorced six months ago, and until then they had run a cybersecurity business as a team. When they divorced, Lara sold her interest to him."

"Was it an amicable split?"

"Not at all. Charles, her ex, fought like hell against the property division. Claimed Lara had inflated the value of the business just to screw with him. Even though Charles had selected the appraiser they used. Finally, Lara signed over her half of the house gratis, just to be rid of the aggravation."

"What did she get for the business?"

"Twenty million. But only ten of that up front."

"Why?"

"Charles said a payout that large would make it impossible to stay in business. He proposed royalties to cover half. Lara agreed because that would give her an income and allow her to invest the ten million in another venture. She had thought of opening a center for the arts. A bookstore. A gallery. Something to feed the soul, she said."

"What's the royalty?"

"$500,000, annually."

Gabe whistled. "For how long?"

"Lara said the royalty was for life, until paid in full. I have a copy of the agreement if you want to see it."

Gabe had stalled back at "for life."

"The royalty ended with Lara's death?"

"Yes." Quinn shook her head. "I know where you're going, but it's a lucrative business. The royalty was probably a quarter of its profits. I can't see Charles killing her over that."

Gabe made a note in his book to check out the business and Charles.

"What's his last name? Charles."

"Michelson. Lives in Vancouver."

Gabe jotted that down. Then he asked, "Did Lara leave a will?"

"Yes, but only because I harped at her until she did so. She's two years older than me, but much younger in her outlook. She was healthy and believed wills were for the older set." Quinn sighed. "Luckily, I convinced her to get a will done. I'm the executor and the primary beneficiary. I can give you a copy if you like?"

"Yeah, let me have a copy of the royalty agreement and her will. Also, contact information for Charles if you have it."

Quinn reached into her bag and extracted some documents. "I guessed you'd want to see everything," she said, passing them over to Gabe. "Do you want me to sign a contract?"

Gabe said, "I'll email you one. My rate is $150 an hour. I usually ask for a retainer, but since you're a judge and I know where to find you, I'll waive that. I will report daily, even if it's only to say, 'nothing new to report.' Does that sound doable?"

"Sounds perfect." Quinn tasted a forkful of the maple sugar pie, and a smile split her face. "As perfect as this pie."

21

When the Helper Was Sixteen
ONTARIO

THE BOY ENTERED the guidance counselor's office at four o'clock on the dot. "Hi, Mrs. Heinz."

She smiled at him and gestured to the chair in front of her desk. "Right on time, as usual. Have a seat." She gestured at the metal chair in front of her desk.

The boy lowered his tall frame onto the chair and crossed one jean-clad leg over the other.

"I have some brochures for you," Mrs. Heinz said, "about different career paths you might consider. Have you thought about what you'd like to do after high school?"

He shrugged a typical high schooler's shrug. "Maybe travel? School's okay, but I feel like I'll need a break from it."

"A gap year is a good idea. But have you asked your social worker whether the foster care program will give you any financial assistance if you aren't in school?"

"Not yet, but I will." He shrugged again. "I don't mind working while I travel. Maybe I could get a job as a tour guide."

"That's an idea," Mrs. Heinz said. "We can explore other options over the next while. It's never too early to plan for your future!"

As if he hadn't thought about his future. He'd been fending for himself since he was eleven. Even before that, really, because Mom was such a mess.

"How are things at home?" Mrs. Heinz asked. "Any problems?"

"Nah. The Samsons are okay foster parents. Boring actually. But don't tell them I said that."

She looked relieved. He knew what she was thinking. Boring was good when it came to foster care. Better than the horror stories some kids lived through. Still, his life was its own type of lonely horror. The Samsons gave him food, a place to sleep, and a small allowance. That was it. No hugs, smiles, conversation. They paid more attention to their lampshades than to him. Sometimes he wished they'd yell, or hit him, just so he'd know they felt *something* for him.

Mrs. Heinz handed him the brochures she had mentioned. "Have a look through these and if something piques your interest, we can discuss it."

He smiled at her. "Sure thing, thanks."

He tossed the brochures in the first trash can he passed after he left the school grounds. His mother had always said the future was in the hands of karma. He believed her. Karma was going to get even with all the people who had ruined his life. The judge, his father's idiot lawyer, the jury, the key witness, the prosecutor. Every one of them had conspired to set his father up and send him to jail. Where he died. Every one of them was to blame for his mother hitting the bottle and deciding life was not worth living. And for the fluke that tossed him from the car when she drove it off the road, saving his life. His cruddy life of nothingness.

So far karma was sitting on its hands. None of those people had suffered since his father's trial. No loved ones being ripped unfairly from their lives. Mom said karma would take care of them all. But when?

He had a plan, however. When he'd been eight a woman

in a fancy car had parked in a spot that his mom was waiting for. "Well look at that," Mom said. "I have my blinker on, and she knows damn well that's our spot."

Mom had parked several rows away from the woman. As they walked toward the mall Mom spotted a short screw on the ground. She giggled and picked it up. "Sometimes," she said, "karma needs a little help."

His mother scraped the screw along the side of the woman's car. Then she placed it, pointed end up, behind one of the car's rear tires. "Sure hope she knows how to change a flat," Mom said.

So yeah, he'd wait till after high school. If karma hadn't got around to fixing things by then, he'd head west and give karma a helping hand.

22

Sunday, July 18, 2010
SILVERTON LAKE, NEAR CHEAKAMUS, B.C.

MID-MORNING ON SUNDAY, Gabe pulled his F150 into a spacious parking spot near the concession stand at Silverton Lake, hoping to grab a coffee before he checked out Watercraft U-Rent.

There was only one other vehicle in the lot, a dented blue Honda Civic with a missing rear bumper and an oxidized paint job. Any other Sunday in the middle of summer, Gabe suspected, this lot would be jammed with vehicles and the beach would be awash in umbrellas and suntan oil. But Friday's sailing accident had evidently put a pall on the beachgoing crowd. Probably many of them had opted to spend this particular Sunday in church, offering gratitude that they had not been in that ill-fated boat.

He jumped from the truck, clicked the lock, and strode around the small building to the front. Where the shutters were in place over the windows. Where a sign full of curlicues and hearts said, "So sorry to have missed you. On vacay. Back July 19."

Well hell. He'd woken up this morning with a headache. He'd been running late so didn't stop by Tiffany's for his usual Prince of Darkness, a blend guaranteed to shake those cobwebs and dull thuds out of his head. Gabe had counted on a coffee at the lake to take care of what ailed him, at least temporarily, so he could get his day back on track.

And now this inconsiderate person says, "so sorry?" Even with a heart accompanying it, "so sorry" wouldn't cut it. What concessioner closed their stand in the middle of summer to go on "vacay?" Why couldn't they have hired a couple of high schoolers to dispense the coffee and hamburgers while they wandered off on their heart-and-curlicued vacay?

Gabe turned toward the lake and scanned the area. Empty lifeguard stand. A floating dock about a hundred feet offshore, with two aluminum ladders offering access to swimmers. Also empty. And five hundred feet, give or take, to his left, an array of the smallest sailboats he'd ever seen sat at the edge of the lake, anchored by ropes to a stanchion on the beach.

When Judge Quinn said her sister had been sailing, he had envisioned a boat that would be sea-worthy. These boats looked like rowboats with a sail. Lara Quinn went up in Gabe's estimation when he realized she'd been in one of these teeny sardine cans. With not even a cabin below where she could make a coffee. Lordy.

He trudged across the sand to the sailboats and approached a small, colorful shack. On the sand outside the shack, a young guy in shorts and a tank top stood with his back to Gabe. He wore heavy duty earphones over his ears and swiped at the body of a dinghy with a paintbrush. As he got closer, Gabe noticed splotches of white paint on the sand near the boat. And more of them on the guy's tanned legs.

"Morning," Gabe said.

The fellow kept on swiping.

Gabe raised his voice. "Morning."

More swiping. Christ, how loud was the kid's music? He was gonna be deaf before he was thirty.

Gabe tapped the painter on his shoulder. Immediately the swiping was replaced by a shriek, a loose-limbed leap upward, and a paint can somersaulting through the air. Gabe jumped back to avoid the ribbons of white paint spiraling behind the tumbling can. He made a note to file this under, "Greeting strangers, how not to."

The guy ripped his earphones from his head and turned to face Gabe. "Jeeezusssss!"

"Sorry man," Gabe said. "I should have approached you from the front."

"You think?" The guy bent over, put his hands on his knees, and sucked in a deep breath. "Oh man, I thought I was about to die. I was listening to *The Shining*. Really into it. And Jack was just outside the door."

"That would do it." Gabe pointed at the paint can, now upended on the sand about thirty feet away. "I think I owe you a can of paint. And I can help you clean the spills from the sand."

When the fellow removed his Ray-Bans and ran his hand through his long hair, Gabe recognized the surfer dude who'd been in Tiffany's the day before.

Surfer dude said, "S'okay. I have a shack full of paint, and it won't take long to scoop it out of the sand. Wanna rent a boat?"

"Nah. My name's Gabe. I wanted to talk to you about the day that woman died out here in the lake. Her sister asked me to get some more details about what happened."

The fellow shook Gabe's hand and said, "Connor. Yeah, I don't know too much 'cause I had an appointment that morning and closed the store for a few hours. I rented her this boat and said she could just pull it up here when she was done and leave it if I wasn't back."

"You didn't worry about leaving the lake with her out there?"

Connor kicked at the sand. "No man, y'know. She said she had been sailing all her life. No prob, she said. And y'know, I hadda go."

And Connor was probably high. His appointment was probably to get more dope. Gabe let it slide. "This is the boat she rented?"

Connor patted the hull of the boat he'd been painting. "Yep. Dinghy Boat number one."

Gabe had been right. A rowboat with a sail. He strolled around the boat. "Where's the sail and boom thingy?"

"Beside the shack. I removed them so I could repaint the body."

"Did you notice anything on the boom, like a mark where it hit her? Can I have a look?"

Connor led Gabe to the side of the shack where the boom and sail were stashed. Gabe ran his hand over the surface of the boom, hoping to feel a dent. Nothing. "Don't suppose the cops found any hair or…um, other evidence, on it?" he asked.

"You mean like blood? Or brains?" Connor shook his head. "Nah. The boom isn't heavy enough to do that kind of damage. When it hits someone, it can bruise them. Or stun them. The biggest risk is that it can knock the sailor into the water."

Gabe nodded. "So, were you the one who found her?"

"Oh yeah, man. It was gruesome. I got back here from my errand and saw the boat was still on the lake. And that made me wonder, because it was raining like stink and I couldn't believe she'd still be out there."

Connor gazed at the lake for a moment and then went on. "Then I realized there was no one actually *in* the boat. I hopped on the Seadoo and went out there. And there she was, floating, face down. I phoned 911 right away, got her out of the water into the boat. I tried CPR but no joy. So I towed the boat back to the shore and waited on the emergency guys."

"You notice anything in the boat itself? Anything out of place?"

Connor gazed skyward and pursed his lips. Then he said, "Nothing out of place. Unless you count the life vest."

"What about it?"

"It was in the cockpit. She'd taken it off. Which was weird."

"Why's that?"

"Because I never rent a boat to anyone unless they agree to wear a life vest. I made a point of telling her because the weather looked iffy. And she told me not to worry. She joked she would even wear a life vest 24/7 on a cruise liner."

"Huh."

Gabe thought about what Connor had told him. Over all, not much, except to confirm Judge Quinn's statement that Lara was safety conscious.

"What about the lifeguard?" he asked.

"Only on weekends," Connor said.

"And the concession people?"

"Vacay."

"Right. Okay, Connor, thanks for talking with me. Sorry again about the scare I gave you."

Gabe was halfway back across the beach when Connor shouted. "Hey, wait up! There was one other weird thing."

23

Sunday, July 18, 2010

THE PEAK BAR

EARLY SUNDAY AFTERNOON, Gabe pulled another two Irish coffee glasses from the shelves and set them next to the ten already on the bar. A dozen of them now sat in a straight line, sparkling under the lights. He imagined each glass shooting sparks into the ether, eagerly expecting the cheerful ping the sugar cube would make as it cleared the rim and landed inside the glass. The first sign of the lip-smacking concoction soon to turn an empty container into a vessel holding warmth and comfort.

He grabbed the box of sugar cubes from beneath the bar and walked the length of the aisle behind the bar to a spot five feet from the first of the glasses. The last glass in the line sat approximately ten feet away from Gabe. He selected four cubes from the box, holding them in his left hand. Setting the box on the bar, he rolled his shoulders to loosen up, rocked his neck back and forth twice, planted his feet solidly, and breathed in quietly. He transferred one cube to his right hand, breathed in again, and tossed. Ping! If this had been basket-ball, the customers at the bar would have heard the swish of the net. Instead, they merely heard the tinkle as the cube hit the bottom inside of the glass and ricocheted three times before settling at rest.

A fellow halfway down the bar groaned. "I gather you chose this day in the pool, eh, Vic?" Gabe asked.

"Yeah," Vic said. "Have pity Gabe, I really want to retire early and the When-Will-Gabe-Miss-a-Shot pool is my only hope."

Gabe tossed a second cube. Ping, followed by Vic's groan.

And so it went, ten more cubes tossed, ten more pings and ten more groans. Throughout, Gabe was in auto mode, tossing cubes, but thinking about what he'd learned from Connor at Silverton Lake a few hours ago. Specifically, that Connor had been painting the boat because Lara Quinn had vandalized it, using a permanent marker to change the number "1" on the boat's hull to "7." And then printing a word beside the number. The word "karma."

"Total drag man," Connor had said. "Usually, we only repaint the boats at the end of each season, and that one was still looking superb, y'know? And it's hard to cover black marker with white. I was on the second coat when you happened by."

Why would Lara bother to vandalize the boat? Then again, was it Lara? Connor admitted he hadn't noticed anything on the boat when he hauled it to the shore. "But hey, it was raining like mad, and I was totally freaked out. I mean, there was a dead woman there, right? And I was focusing on getting her back into the sailboat. And then doing CPR 'cause I thought maybe she wasn't dead, or I could bring her back, y'know? And then I had to tow the boat in. I mean, there coulda been something there, but I wasn't looking. Or maybe it happened overnight, after everyone left. I just don't know, man."

Yep, Connor had definitely been high.

"Was the graffiti smudged or streaked?" Gabe asked.

"Nope."

If Lara Quinn had marked up the boat, she must have done it well before the rainstorm started.

"Did you find a marker in the boat?" he asked Connor.

"No, but y'know I gotta think that someone who would vandalize a boat wouldn't worry too much about tossing stuff into the lake."

Gabe tended to agree with Connor. Then he asked whether the cops or paramedics had said anything about graffiti. "Well, duh, man. If they had, I woulda noticed it then, wouldn't I?"

Well, given Connor's probable state of mind, maybe not.

Most likely the whole thing was a red herring. Some teenager fooling around—a graffiti lover, just like Gabe's younger brother Jack had been last year. That was the thing with graffiti, however, sometimes it meant something. What was it this time? Meaningful, or a prank?

After he tossed, and sank, his final sugar cube, Gabe delivered a pint of draft to Vic at the bar. "Sorry, not sorry, you didn't win the pool. Have a beer on me."

After cleaning the Irish coffee glasses and removing the sugar cubes from the bar, Gabe grabbed his cell phone and shot a text to Jack.

> Hey Jacko. Do u know a tagger named karma? Does karma mean anything special in the tagging world?

A minute later, his phone chimed. Jacko texted:

> No to both. How's the knee, greenhorn? Wanna try bull riding next?

Before Gabe could text back, Maxine Lanning rapped her knuckles on the bar. "Barkeep, barkeep. A glass of your finest red for your favorite reporter."

When Gabe delivered the wine to Maxine, he said, "You know you're the *only* reporter in town, right?"

Maxine grinned. "I was speaking in the universal sense. Any juicy tidbits you can share with me? Tidbits to spice up tomorrow's copy?"

Gabe wiped down the counter in front of Maxine. He wouldn't mind kicking the whole vandalism thing around with her. She was sharp and more than once had got his brain cells churning in a completely different, and worthwhile, direction. But he hadn't yet called Judge Quinn to fill her in on what Connor had told him. It would not be good for the Judge to read about her sister vandalizing a boat before Gabe told her.

"Not on the record," he said. "Gotta talk to someone beforehand."

Maxine said, "No issue with that. You know I can keep things quiet when needed. Just let me know when the embargo's lifted."

"Fair enough. I was at Silverton Lake today chatting with the young guy who manages the boat rental place."

"Uh-huh. And?"

Gabe summarized his conversation with Connor, ending with, "And according to Connor, Lara, or someone else vandalized the sailboat."

"Vandalized? Like chopping a hole in the bottom?"

"No. Like using a black marker to change the number from one to seven and to add the word 'karma' beside the number."

Maxine's eyes widened and her wineglass slipped from her grip, clattering on the bar top, its contents splashing across the surface and onto Gabe's apron.

Gabe noticed she was shaking. "Maxine? Are you okay? What's wrong?"

"Stay there. Stay right there. I will be back. There's something I have to show you."

24

Sunday, July 18, 2010
CHEAKAMUS, B.C.

THE HELPER SAT on an idling ATV at Deception Ridge viewpoint on Rimrock Mountain. He pulled his bush hat lower to shade his eyes from the sun and turned off the ignition. He needed silence to think about something that could be a major problem.

He'd seen the friggin judge in the café with Gabrieli. She had hired him!

It wasn't optimum to have a detective snooping around.

Still, how good a detective could a bartender be? All Gabrieli seemed to do was toss sugar cubes at empty glasses, and sit in Tiffany's chowing down.

Apparently, the judge didn't believe the sailing accident was an accident. The Helper thought back over that day at the lake. Karma had been sending good luck his way. First, Lara Quinn shows up in Cheakamus to visit her sister. That saved The Helper a trip to Vancouver and the challenge of creating an accident in the city.

Second, no one else had been at Silverton Lake when he killed Lara Quinn. She was out there on the lake, alone in her rented sailboat. The weather had started out calmly, but a storm moved in, pelting the lake with rain. As he expected, when the weather worsened, she lowered the sail, grabbed her oars, and pointed the boat toward the shore.

He had tossed his bat into a dinghy, pushed off, and rowed toward her. She obviously thought he was coming to help because when he shouted at her, she looked over her shoulder and smiled.

He could not have planned it better. When his dinghy was within arm's reach, she let go of an oar and leaned toward him to grab his gunwale. He snatched up his bat and swung it, smacking the back of her head. Stunned, she fell forward, partway into his dinghy.

He pushed her away and watched her fall headfirst into the water. Then it was a simple matter of holding her head under water until she drowned. He made sure she was dead, like he should have done with Stillwater. Then he removed her life vest and tossed it into the sailboat's cockpit.

He left her, floating but dead, while he secured his dinghy to her sailboat. He climbed aboard, put the oars back into the oarlocks, and raised the sail. Once that was done, he climbed back into the dinghy, untethered it, and rowed to shore, where he returned the boat to its original spot. He grabbed his bat and left the lake.

Later that night, after the police and others had left, he returned to the lake with a black marker and printed his message on the sailboat's hull.

He was positive no one had seen him at the lake either time. He was equally sure that no one suspected he was anything other than a young guy holding down a job that didn't interfere with his desire to enjoy life in the mountains. Pleasant, easy going, unthreatening. He'd worked hard all his life at being what people expected, and he was thankful for that practice because it was difficult to control his emotions in Cheakamus. Seeing those evil people going about their day, in Tiffany's or The Peak Bar, or strolling around town. He wanted to get in their faces and scream at them. Say, "Look at me! I'm all that's left. You took my family away from me. I was happy once and you ruined it."

Instead, he put on a bland face, nodded and chatted and smiled. Just another guy hanging out. No one had a clue about the agony roiling around just below the surface. Least of all Gabrieli.

The Helper nodded to himself and smacked the ATV handles. People shouldn't mess with karma. Gabrieli shouldn't mess with karma. How would the private eye like it if he lost someone he loved? Maybe the guy needed a lesson.

The Helper added Gabrieli's brother to his list.

25

Sunday, July 18, 2010
THE PEAK BAR

WHEN MAXINE RUSHED BACK into The Peak, she was puffing and red in the face. She slid onto a stool at the far end of the bar, well away from other patrons, and motioned Gabe over. He poured a glass of red wine, and another of water, and took them to her.

"Did you run all the way? You look like you could use this water."

She nodded and gasped. "Yes, thanks." She chugged the water. "Do you know how far it is from here to the office and back?"

"Two blocks. You're out of shape."

"Two *long, uphill* blocks. Both ways." She pulled two sheets of paper from her jacket pocket. "Look at these," she said, handing them to Gabe.

Gabe shuffled the papers, noticing that the text on each one began with "Dear Editor." He read the first one silently:

"Dear Editor, The obituary about the pitiful excuse for a lawyer, Hugo Driesden, didn't mention a few things. Like how he deserved to die a much more painful death than he did. Like how he's a lucky man that his heart cratered before The Helper arrived. It was coming. Karma never forgets."

"Weird," Gabe said, setting the piece of paper on the bar. He turned his attention to the second letter to the editor, a short two lines long:

"Dear Editor, Those people in the Winnebago didn't go off the road by accident. It was Karma."

"When did you get these?" Gabe asked Maxine, handing the letters back to her.

"The first one, the one about the RV, came in not long after the Wurtzes drove off the road. I figured it was a nasty prank and didn't print it."

Gabe tapped the second letter. "And this one?"

"That arrived a week ago. Again, I thought it was some prankster. But I decided to stop the idiot from delivering any more letters."

Gabe nodded. "Right. I remember your editorial about anonymous fools expecting to take up valuable space in the paper but not being brave enough to sign their names. Was that spurred by these letters?"

"For sure. And I thought it worked because so far, they haven't sent another one in. But now…"

"Now, there's the same word on a sailboat where a woman died."

26

Sunday, July 18, 2010
ROCQUE & HOUND GUESTHOUSE, CHEAKAMUS

Gabe had discovered the wonders of Sunday dinners not long after he had formally decided to continue living in Cheakamus, when Greta had invited him to dinner one Sunday. He was one of ten people at that dinner. Eleven if you counted his god-daughter Devon snoozing in her carrier. Roast beef with Yorkshire pudding and all the trimmings. Trifle for dessert. The meal was a nod to Greta's mother, who had grown up in Britain. "Except that my roast beef is sumptuous," Greta said. "Whereas my mother believed a perfectly done roast meant leaving it in the oven one hour past very well-done."

Getting the dinner on the table was a group effort. Greta enlisted guests to slice bread, mash potatoes, stir gravy, steam vegetables, and set the table. Everyone earned their right to enjoy the main course and dessert, and to treat themselves to seconds.

Sunday dinners when Gabe was growing up were the same as dinner any other night of the week±haphazard, often leftovers, more often takeout from the burger stand, and sometimes a frozen pizza fired into the oven.

During that first dinner at Greta's house, Gabe listened to

the chatter of multiple conversations taking place simultaneously, joined in toasts and laughter, and watched the happy and smiling faces of the people around the table. The day's tensions evaporated, and he reveled in the feeling that, on this day at least, his often chaotic world was calm and secure. He filed the sensation under "family, belonging."

Tonight, Sunday dinner with his favorite landlady awaited. Just the two of them, but no less special than that first one months ago.

After he fed the cat, Gabe showered, shaved, and changed into a clean pair of jeans and his gray cashmere sweater. The one Bethany had given him. The one that led to one of their most loving nights.

He glanced at his watch. He needed to be at Greta's door in two minutes. Plenty of time, seeing as her back door was at the end of a short garden path from her garage, above which his apartment sat.

Doofus wove his body around and between Gabe's legs, purring. "I'd take you with me to Greta's, Doofus. But you know her pooch is scared of you. You gotta hang out here."

Gabe opened the slider, stepped onto his balcony, and breathed in, hoping for a hint of tonight's menu. Instead, he smelled sweet peas and roses. Not one whiff of dinner.

He hurried down the stairs and out the door, and picked his way along the garden path. He stopped long enough to pick a handful of fragrant sweet peas. Greta's tomatoes were in full bloom. He wondered if there was some Italian in her DNA because she had a knack and a love for growing tomatoes.

He managed to get both feet on Greta's porch and raise his hand to knock before Greta opened the door and waved him inside. They should run another pool at Tiffany's: "When Will Gabe Knock on Greta's Door Before She Opens It?"

He passed the sweet peas to Greta. "I picked some wildflowers for you."

Greta snorted. "These look remarkably like the ones in my garden."

"You bet. If anything, I know where to find the best flowers." Gabe sniffed the air in the kitchen. Fresh bread. His mouth watered. Then he detected pot roast. He groaned with pleasure.

"Why the groan?" Greta asked. "Is your knee still bothering you? What are you doing wrestling steers, anyway? You're not young anymore, you know."

"What do you mean, I'm not young? Isn't forty the new twenty? And I'm not yet forty, so I'm a mere kid. I was groaning because I smell your delicious pot roast. And I've been saving my appetite all day just for this moment."

Gabe extracted plates and glasses from the cabinets. Then he opened the second drawer next to the sink and chose cutlery. Fork, knife, soup spoons. He set the table and then relaxed in the chair nearest the range. A fellow could never be too close to pot roast.

Greta handed him a bread knife. "Cut some bread for us, will you, while I get the dinner from the oven?" She glanced at the table settings. "We won't need the spoons. It's so much better to sop up the gravy with bread."

As he sliced the bread, Gabe said, "Yeah, I agree. But all the extra goodies in your pot roast need a spoon."

After Gabe had finished his first serving of pot roast, spending most of that time groaning with delight as he scooped potatoes, carrots, turnip, and a few other tasty vegetables he didn't recognize into his soup spoon, he said, "I need to run something by you, Greta."

"Sure. Do you want more pot roast?"

"Well, duh. But in a minute. First, let me tell you about my day." Gabe told Greta about his trip to Silverton Lake, the conversation with Connor, and the revelations from Maxine.

"Do I know this Connor?" Greta asked.

"He's a young guy running the sailboat rentals at Silverton

Lake," Gabe said. "About twenty maybe. Looks like he'd rather be surfing. Longish hair, permanent Ray-Bans. I don't think he's a local. He could be merely working here for the summer."

Gabe took a sip of water. "I called Judge Quinn earlier and told her about the graffiti on the sailboat. She couldn't say that Lara would never do such a thing, but she said they didn't share everything and after years on the bench, she knew everyone had secrets. Then I texted Jack, and he said karma means nothing to him, at least in terms of graffiti artists."

"It's weird," Greta said.

"No kidding. What have you heard about it?"

Greta said, "Nothing about the sailing accident itself, other than what a tragedy it is. But some people have commented on the two deadly accidents. They're worried about Wilfred Stillwater's accident too."

"There does seem to be a cluster of them, hey? I wonder whether the graffiti 'Karma #7' on the sailboat means some-thing. Or am I seeing boogie men where there aren't any?"

"I had heard that there was a slip of paper in Leonard Wurtz's RV that mentioned karma. But Stan Wurtz told me he assumed his mother had found a new subject to research. She was always looking at the fantastical—witches, fairies, guardian angels she believed they all existed. Karma would be something that would appeal to her."

"Uh-huh." Gabe reached for the casserole dish and ladled another serving of pot roast onto his plate. He selected a thick slice of bread and buttered it.

"Suppose," he said, as he dipped the bread into the gravy swimming on his plate. "Suppose 'Karma #7' means seven deaths?"

He ticked the names off on his fingers. "I've got the Wurtzes, so that's two. Then Lara Quinn makes three. And let's say the second letter to the editor about Driesden, the lawyer, counts in the killer's head. That makes four."

Greta nodded. "Correct. You are missing three."

"Right. That's what I come up with too."

Gabe scooped up the last morsel of roast and potato, popped it into his mouth, and chewed slowly. When he swallowed, he said, "Your pot roast beats anything at Tiffany's. But don't tell Rhonda I said that. She will ban me for sure."

He wiped his mouth with his napkin. "What does Lara Quinn have in common with Driesden and the Wurtzes?"

Greta said, "Other than they are all dead, not much that I can see. Driesden lived in Trail, the Wurtzes were from Cheakamus, and Lara Quinn lived in Vancouver."

"Driesden was a lawyer," Gabe said. "Quinn worked in cybersecurity. And the Wurtzes were retired. Before retirement, old man Wurtz was an accountant who mostly did tax returns and farm accounting for locals."

"You are going to have to look into their backgrounds," Greta said.

"If the word 'karma' means anything, there must be a connection. And I can't ignore the fact that the word has cropped up in three local deaths. Another thing worrying me is this: suppose it's not seven historical deaths. Suppose Lara was merely #7 on a list and this guy is dispensing with his victims out of order, randomly?"

"Oh no," Greta said. "In that case…"

"Who's next?"

27

Monday, July 19, 2010
THE PEAK BAR

Early Monday morning, Gabe opened The Peak Bar and began readying it for the day's patrons. As he emptied the commercial dishwasher, he thought again about the weirdness of the word "karma" appearing in connection with three deaths around Cheakamus. Could it be a mere coincidence? Or an opportunistic prankster?

And if not, if the references to karma were intentional, was there a killer in the town who might be targeting others?

Gabe pulled his small black notebook from his jeans' back pocket, grabbed a pen, and thumbed to clean pages. At the top of the first two pages, he added the headings "Leonard Wurtz" and "Verna Wurtz" and beneath, jotted down "motives" and "suspects." Under those subheadings, Gabe entered question marks.

He flicked to the following page, where he added the heading "Lara Quinn," and the same two sub-headings. Under "motives," he inserted "divorce." Under the suspects heading, he added "ex."

Gabe titled the third page "Driesden." Under both the motives and suspects sub-headings Gabe wrote "criminal defense lawyer." If he exhausted all other avenues, Gabe would look into Driesden's past cases, but he knew that would take massive hours of research. A better use of his time would be to focus on the Wurtzes and Lara Quinn.

Thinking about the karma references reminded Gabe of his text exchange with Jack. It had been more than a week since he'd spent time with his younger brother, so he sent a quick text:

"Hey Jacko. Lunch on Saturday? My treat."

Immediately came the response:

"UR on bro Tiffany's @ noon."

Gabe knew exactly what Jack, being as addicted to Rhonda's secret sauce as Gabe, would order at the café: double cheeseburger and fries. Unless the menu offered poutine as a side.

The Peak was ready for customers. Glasses and pint mugs were clean and within easy reach; tables had been wiped down; condiments refreshed on the tables; overhead television screens tuned to a sports channel. Perhaps he had time to dig into the question of motives for someone to kill Quinn or the Wurtzes.

Gabe had read Lara Quinn's will, and it confirmed that Judge Quinn was the principal beneficiary, after a bequest to a charity focusing on early readers. The divorce settlement was also as the Judge had described it—the residence to Charles, the business split evenly with Charles paying Lara twenty million. That amount was to be paid ten million up front, and the balance by annual royalties from the business.

As for the royalty agreement, it stipulated that Lara would receive a payment of $500,000 annually from the cybersecurity business until the remaining ten million was paid in full, or until her death, whichever happened first.

Judge Quinn had been adamant that Charles would not kill Lara simply because of the ongoing royalty commitment. However, the agreement also stated that the royalty was attached to the business, moving with it if Charles sold out.

Gabe thought about the business deals he had handled as a lawyer. Royalties were like an ongoing debt for the company. If Charles sold the business, the royalty wouldn't end. It would continue, be a debt that the new owners had to honor. That could affect the sale value of the company. And that might be sufficient to make Charles think about how much better off he'd be if Lara died.

Gabe placed a call to Charles Michelson in Vancouver. When he was bumped to voice mail, Gabe introduced himself and then said, "Lara's sister has asked me to investigate Lara's death. I'd appreciate any information you can share that will help in my investigation." Best to avoid the question 'Did you off your ex?' in the first interaction with Michelson.

Then Gabe phoned Stan Wurtz and, after the initial pleasantries, asked, "Are you still going through your parents' belongings?"

Stan sighed into the phone. "So far, nothing has popped up. My parents led a good, but uneventful, life. I haven't found a thing in Dad's files or on his computer—no threats, no complaints from old clients."

"Huh," Gabe said. "Did you check your mother's things?"

"You've got to be kidding, Gabe. Who would want to kill my mother? It was my father who had the sedative in his system, remember."

"Yeah, but your mother didn't drive, did she? I'm just thinking the person would know that."

Stan was silent for a beat. "Mom was all about helping others. She did good. She wasn't a woman who would stir up trouble."

"I thought that's what you'd say, but it never hurts to ask."

Gabe was about to end the call when Stan said, "Except…"

"Except what?" Gabe asked.

"Except the food bank. A couple years ago Mom was secretary of the food bank society. She told me she thought the treasurer was skimming. She wanted me to audit the books."

"Did you?"

"No, I'm not a forensic accountant. The only experience I've had with that sort of thing was at an old job when I discovered someone fooling around with the accounts. Had to testify in the court case and after the abuse the defense lawyer heaped on me, I vowed never to get involved like that again. I told Mom to report her suspicions to the head of the organization."

"Do you know what happened?"

"No, sorry."

Gabe got contact information for the food bank from Stan and was about to phone the number when Harris entered the bar. He looked tired.

As Harris poured himself a glass of beer, Gabe filled him in on his worries that there could be a killer stalking townspeople.

Harris frowned. "This whole mess is another reason we need to get moving on setting up our own police force. Hunting for a Police Chief is exhausting work. Just reading the mountains of resumés makes my eyes sting."

"Any worthwhile prospects?" Gabe asked.

"Three so far. I'm interviewing two of them by video conference because they live in Ontario. The third one wants to come here to check out the town and meet me in person."

"That's a good sign, isn't it? That they want to get a sense of the town?"

Harris nodded and took a few steps toward his office at the

back of the bar before turning around. "Hey, remember Wilfred Stillwater? The fellow who fell out of his truck in the casino parking lot? I heard some guy tried to kill him last Thursday."

Gabe stopped hunting for his box of sugar cubes and stared at Harris. "Is he okay?"

"Oh, yeah. And now they have a guard outside his hospital room."

"What happened?"

"I didn't get any details. All I know is the guy got away, and the cops are on the hunt."

"Jeez, where's LeBlanc when we need him, hey? Off having a great time with Lucy in Toronto."

"I didn't know Lucy was there too," Harris said. "I thought she hated Toronto."

"She does." Gabe shook his head. "I don't know about this one. Usually, Lucy's so coolheaded when it comes to men. This time seems different. She's gotta have it bad if she's willing to sweat it out in Hogtown just to spend time with LeBlanc."

"It's probably the uniform. It does something to women's libido. I remember when Kate and I went to the wedding of a constable in LeBlanc's detachment. All the men in the wedding party, and several of the male guests, wore the Mountie red serge dress uniform. Kate could not take her eyes off them, and when LeBlanc asked her to dance, I thought she'd swoon."

Harris thought for a moment and then grinned. "I gotta say that night we had the best sex ever. To the point where I thought about calling the RCMP recruiters."

"I don't believe you."

"Yeah, okay, I never seriously considered joining the force. But I bought a Mountie costume for Halloween. And you know, I'm pretty sure we conceived Devon the night of that wedding."

Gabe stared at his friend. "My goddaughter? My goddaughter was conceived with the help of the Mounties? Geez, Harris, you could have spared me this information. It's right up there with finding out your parents actually had sex."

Harris grinned. "Lemme know if you ever want to borrow the costume."

28

Monday, July 19, 2010
SILVERTON HOSPITAL

Gabe stuck his head inside the door of *The Journal's* office. The receptionist, a middle-aged woman wearing her mousy brown hair in a topknot, peered at him from her metal desk. Gabe noticed a pencil sticking out of her bun. The pencil bore a small sticky note with the word "WHAT," followed by two question marks, scratched on it in enormous red letters.

"Is Maxine around?" Gabe said, answering her unspoken "What?"

"Max!" the woman shouted over her shoulder in the gravelly voice of a former smoker. "Someone here for you."

"Great intercom system," Gabe said with a grin.

She barely glanced up from her computer. "Works for us. Cheap too."

When Maxine entered the small reception area and saw Gabe, she smiled. "Hey, Gabe. Wanna place an ad?"

"Nope. Wondering if you have time to take a ride with me?"

The receptionist said, "Go for it, Max. He looks safe enough, and dates have been scarce for you lately."

Maxine laughed. "Have you met Josephine Carter? My

receptionist, proofreader, lonely hearts advisor, and general pain in the ass?"

"Sorry to disappoint you, Josephine," Gabe said, "not a date. Maxine and I need to visit a friend in the hospital."

Josephine let out a theatrical sigh. "Honest to Pete, men these days. It's like you all lost sight of what the world needs. Romance. It needs romance. Maybe a bit of sex thrown in there. Or the other way around. A lot of sex, with a hint of romance. In my day, it was a whole different story."

She sucked in a breath, but before she could launch into what Gabe was sure would be a tale of torrid bodice-ripping sex, Maxine interrupted.

"Let me grab my bag and I'll meet you outside."

Gabe said, "Bring a recorder too, eh?" He nodded at Josephine. "Glad to know someone is looking out for Maxine's best interests."

"Damn tooting I am."

When Maxine settled in the passenger seat of Gabe's truck, she said, "Who's the friend we're visiting?"

"Wilfred Stillwater. He's in Silverton Hospital."

"The guy in the coma? The one who cracked his head at Silverton Casino?"

"The very one," Gabe said. "Someone tried to kill him Thursday."

"Really? What happened?"

Gabe made a U-turn on Main Street and headed west toward Silverton. "Dunno. That's why we're going to visit him. Well, he's in a coma, so I guess we'll have to visit the nurses. I heard there's a police guard outside his room, which may create some challenges."

"And you want me to charm the cop, distract him with my feminine beauty?"

"Nuh-uh. Not that I doubt your ability to do so, of course."

"Of course."

"I think you will look less threatening to the cop than me. If he's at his station, I will keep him occupied, maybe bribe him with a coffee, while you do all the dirty work."

"Sounds like a good plan." Maxine pulled her notebook from her bag. "Let's make a list of the highlights we want to cover."

———

As THEY WALKED along the hallway toward the elevator in the Silverton Hospital, Gabe tried to shake off the heebie-jeebies that always hit him in hospitals. Was it the lingering scent of rubbing alcohol? Or the squeak of shoes on the tiled floors? Or the beeping of monitors? He shuddered and tried to breathe slowly, willing his heart to beat more slowly and hoping the slight narrowing of his vision was an illusion.

They exited the elevator on the second floor and approached the nurses' station. Gabe noticed three of the patient rooms along the hall had sizable windows into the hallway, allowing staff an easy view of the patients inside. An empty chair sat outside one of those rooms, almost directly across from the nurses' station. That must be Wilfred's room. The cop was hopefully having a break.

At the desk, Gabe stood beside a vase of flowers and inhaled their sweet aroma. Much better than rubbing alcohol.

"Can I help you?" one of the two nurses behind the desk asked. Gabe read her name tag: J. Franson.

Maxine said, "Hi, we wanted to check on Mr. Stillwater's condition. We're friends from Cheakamus and we heard there'd been a kerfuffle here the other day. Is he okay?"

Nurse Franson nodded. "Yes. He's still comatose, however."

"I bet the whole incident was scary," Maxine said. "Were you on duty, then?"

The second nurse approached. "We both were. Who did you say you were?"

Gabe introduced himself. "I run The Peak Bar in Cheakamus. And this is Maxine Lanning."

Maxine said, "I own *The Journal*. Actually, I was thinking I could do an article about the dangers medical staff face every day. And how it's getting worse."

Nurse Franson said, "We can't talk about patients. Privacy issues." She glanced at her co-worker. "Right, Alice?"

Alice said, "True."

"But you could talk about the incident itself," Maxine said, "if we didn't mention the patient's name? My focus would be on the topic of what risks you sometimes must take to do your jobs."

Alice and Franson shared a look and then nodded. "Sounds okay."

Gabe exhaled the breath he'd been holding.

Franson said, "We didn't really see much of the guy—just the back of him as he went through the door into the stairwell. Judging from the speed he ran, he's either an athlete, or under forty-five years old. I tell you, we weren't about to chase him!"

Alice said, "In a big hospital there would be a more secure ICU, and more staff. Here, the best we can do is a few rooms with windows we can peek through. The two of us were dealing with a patient in another room when we heard the alarm from the monitors in Mr. Stillwater's room. Maybe that spooked the guy because he was already sprinting down the hall by the time we ran from the other patient's room to see what was going on. Anyway, when we entered Mr. Stillwater's room, I noticed the IV had been pulled from his arm. The blood pressure monitor had been unplugged. And a pillow was on the floor beside the bed."

"Do you think the guy was trying to smother Wilfred?" Maxine asked.

The nurses nodded. "That's our guess. Mr. Stillwater is comatose, so he couldn't have thrown the pillow down. And neither of us did."

Gabe pointed at the empty chair. "Is that Wilfred's room?"

Franson said, "Yep. We called the police after the whole thing, and they decided a guard might be a good idea. Because even though we cottoned on to things quickly, next time the person might be smarter and not unplug machines with alarms."

Alice said, "Plus, we are a little jittery ourselves. It's nice to have a police presence."

Gabe said, "One last thing. Unplugged monitors, IV, pillow. Anything else weird you noticed?"

They shook their heads. Then Alice said, "Oh, the sign. Weird as heck."

29

Monday, July 19, 2010
CHEAKAMUS, B.C.

GABE SHUCKED HIS JACKET, kicked off his boots, and set his takeout container on the table in his kitchen. His mouth had been watering and his stomach sending "feed me, feed me" signals ever since he collected a double order of Rhonda's spaghetti and meatballs at Tiffany's. The aroma of the rich tomato sauce filled the cab of his truck as he drove the short two blocks home. Now he could smell it wafting through his suite.

Doofus jumped from his nest on the recliner by the balcony slider, stretched luxuriously, and padded over to Gabe. He wove his body around Gabe's legs and then made a beeline for his bowl, where he sat and stared at Gabe. When Gabe didn't immediately produce a tin of cat food, Doofus yowled.

"Yeah, yeah Doofus. I get it. Feed you, feed you. After all, you've had a strenuous day guarding that recliner for me."

Gabe removed two tins of food from the cupboard and showed them to Doofus.

"Beef and gravy?" The cat purred.

"Chicken?" Doofus arched his back and made what sounded like a gag.

Gabe sighed. "It's not like that rooster actually pecked you, Doofus. He got territorial when you wandered into the farmyard. It's been, what, four years since that happened? Pretty sure the threat is over."

Doofus hissed.

"Fine, beef it is. Why do I even ask if you want chicken?"

Once Doofus was fed, Gabe opened his laptop and set it on the kitchen table. Then he opened the takeout container, bent his head over the contents, and inhaled. The aroma conjured visions of olive groves, tomato vines, and cheese vaults. It was like visiting Italy without needing to pack a suitcase. Rhonda, the creator of this masterpiece, had almost been her usual lovingly caustic self lately, which hopefully meant her belief she was "too old for all of this" had been a temporary moment of insanity. Life, without Rhonda as Tiffany's owner, chef, host, and maestro, would be equivalent to drinking a flat beer.

Gabe twirled strands of spaghetti around his fork and popped the bunch into his mouth. He leaned back in his chair, closed his eyes, and chewed, allowing the rich tomato sauce to set his taste buds clamoring for more. Every now and then, Gabe vowed to learn to cook more than grilled steaks and burgers. But then he would have a meal at Greta's or at Tiffany's and decide life was perfect as it was. Why complicate it with cooking lessons?

He pulled his notebook from his pocket and flipped to the notes he'd made about the recent deaths in town. He had four pages devoted to victims so far. Now he added a fifth for Wilfred Stillwater. Possible motives and suspects remained question marks, but Gabe would talk to Wilfred's son, Theo, and with luck, could fill in the blanks.

When Maxine and Gabe had been about to leave Silverton Hospital after their interview with the nurses on Stillwater's floor, Alice, one of the nurses, had mentioned a weird sign in Stillwater's room.

"What sign?" Gabe had asked.

Alice started toward Stillwater's room. "Come and see."

They entered Stillwater's room. Wilfred lay in the hospital bed, his head wrapped in gauze, eyes closed and his body still. "We hope he'll come around in a day or so," Alice said. "There have been some encouraging signs."

She pointed at the wall opposite the bed where a dry erase board was mounted. Scrolled on the board was a message of sorts:

Karma #4 take 2

Gabe snapped a picture with his cell phone, hoping to compare the writing to the sticky note the police found in Leonard Wurtz's RV. If it was a match, he'd know the karma notes weren't coincidences.

On the return trip to Cheakamus, Maxine said, "That sign. Karma #4 take 2. What do you think that means?"

"My guess? The second try at victim number four."

"That sounds like the guy has a list."

"Agreed. Let's keep this karma business under wraps, okay?"

"No prob," Maxine had said. "Won't even share with my bestie, Rhonda."

Now, as Gabe studied his notes and added Stillwater to the list of victims, he again wondered whether the graffiti on Lara's sailboat, "Karma#7," meant she was the seventh victim. Gabe's list in his notebook included Leonard and Verna Wurtz, the lawyer Driesden, Wilfred Stillwater, and Lara Quinn. Five names.

If "Karma#7" meant Lara was the seventh victim, there were two other attacks that had happened and of which Gabe was not aware. Alternatively, perhaps she was number seven on a list that the killer was working his way through randomly.

If so, how long was that list? And who were numbers five and six?

Gabe speared a meatball and counted those remaining in his container. Five. He also had about half of the spaghetti left. Should he save all six meatballs, along with the pasta? He shook his head. Carpe diem.

He reviewed his notes again as he happily chewed the meatball. On the page for Verna Wurtz, he'd made notes about the food bank treasurer that Verna suspected was skimming funds. Grabbing his phone, Gabe called the number Stan had given him for Josie, the woman who was the head of the food bank.

"Josie here," a gravelly voice croaked into the phone.

Gabe introduced himself and before he could launch into the reason for his call, Josie said, "Hey, mister hottie detective, how'd your date go?"

"Pardon?"

She cackled. "With Max. She calls me Josephine, but I prefer Josie." Gabe made the connection. This was the receptionist from *The Journal*.

"Right. Josie, it is. I'm calling about the food bank."

"Need food? Or do you wanna volunteer?"

"I need information." He told her what Stan has mentioned about his mother's suspicions, and then said, "On the QT, Josie, I'm looking into whether anyone had a grudge against Mrs. Wurtz."

"And you thought Patricia, our treasurer, might?" Josie asked.

"Yeah."

"She coulda, I dunno," Josie said. "Last winter Verna told me her suspicions, and I looked into it, and she was right, so I fired Patricia."

"Okay. Where can I find Patricia?"

"Mexico. She moved there three months ago. I heard she's working in a bar and grill on some beach."

Gabe mentally drew a line through Patricia's name. "Thanks, Josie. This helps."

"No sweat. When are you taking Max out again?"

"It wasn't a date."

"Right. Why'd Max look all flushed when she got back to the office then?"

Luckily, Gabe's phone beeped, signaling an incoming call. "Sorry, Josie, I've got another call waiting. Thanks for your help."

"I'll tell Max you were asking about her," Josie said. "Bye, hot stuff."

Gabe pressed the button to accept the call on hold. "Gabrieli," he said.

"Charles Michelson, returning your call," a male voice said.

"Right, thanks. Do you have time to talk to me about your ex-wife?"

"I suppose horrid Kathaleen told you I killed Lara."

Okay, no love lost between the in-laws.

"Actually, no," Gabe said. "She didn't feel you had any reason to. But I wouldn't be doing my job if I didn't check you out, so let me ask you. Did you have anything to do with her death?"

"Of course not. But you'll think I'm lying. What do you need from me as proof?"

"Evidence of your whereabouts over the last two weeks would help. Also, financial records for the business to prove the company could easily afford that royalty."

"Right. I was in Europe for ten days. Just got home yesterday. I will send you flight and hotel confirmation. Ditto financial info."

"Do you have any plans to sell the business in the next while?" Gabe asked.

"And you're thinking the royalty would make a sale difficult?" Charles said. "No, I don't plan to sell, and the royalty is a drop in the bucket compared to our revenues. *And* Lara and I were talking about changing the royalty. Last week, she sent me a note offering to cut it in half."

"Really? Why?"

Gabe could sense Charles' shrug as he said, "Not sure. She said the divorce had given her a new perspective on life."

"Hmmm. What's your take on her death? An unfortunate accident?"

"Nope. Kathaleen and I don't agree on much, but if she thinks Lara's accident was hinky, I'm with her. Lara sailed competitively in university. Maybe if she fell overboard in the Atlantic, she would have died from exposure. But a lake? In the summer, and close to shore? Not a chance. Unless she didn't have a life vest on and was knocked unconscious."

"Lara wasn't wearing a vest."

"Oh, that's totally bizarre. There's no way she'd be sailing without one. Not a big risk taker, Lara. Especially on the water."

"Can you think of anyone who might want to harm Lara? Any past incidents come to mind?"

"Kathaleen comes to mind. Lara called me last Thursday about the royalty. I missed the call, but Lara left a message. Kathaleen had blown her stack when Lara told her what we were discussing. Threats were made."

30

Tuesday, July 20, 2010
SOLOMON'S CHOICE RESORT, NEAR CHEAKAMUS

BEFORE HE POINTED his truck down the highway toward Solomon's Choice Resort, Gabe placed a call to Judge Quinn's clerk and asked for a meeting with Quinn "to discuss developments." The clerk promised to get back to him with details once the judge was done with court for the day.

Gabe hadn't been to Solomon's Choice since last October when he'd been hunting for the saboteurs who were blowing up mining drill rigs. Since then, Etta Clayton and her brother Nestor had teamed up with Theo Stillwater and purchased the resort. Gabe took a moment to look around the area before entering the main lodge. The trio had added additional guest cabins on a ridge, each with a verandah facing the view of nearby mountains. He counted seven new log cabins, gleaming in the hot July sun. That would make fourteen in total. And it appeared that every one of them was occupied at the moment.

On Monday evening, Gabe had phoned Theo Stillwater, Wilfred's son, and asked if they could meet on Tuesday to discuss what happened to Wilfred.

"Morning would be best," Theo said. "In the afternoon

I'll be going to visit Dad at the hospital. Every chance I get I go there to talk to him, hoping he'll hear me and wake up."

Gabe wiped his boots on the mat before entering the lodge. A bell above the door tinkled and a robotic voice said, "Front door open." Gabe strolled across the hardwood planks, heading for the small reception desk tucked discreetly off to the side of the great room. Before he reached it, Etta came around the corner at the back of the room, wiping her hands on a dark green, bibbed apron.

"Gabe! Theo mentioned you'd be by."

"Hey Etta. Yeah, is he around?"

Etta turned and motioned Gabe to follow. "Come to the kitchen. I've got coffee on. Theo's in the barn with Nestor, I think. There's a mare foaling. Let me call him."

After she made the call to the barn, Etta poured a coffee for each of them and joined Gabe at the counter. She pushed a plate of cookies toward him. "Rhonda's got the exclusive on my muffins, but our contract says nothing about cookies. Chocolate chip."

Gabe had eaten three of Etta's mouth-watering cookies when Theo entered the kitchen. Whenever Gabe looked at Theo, he thought about Sequoias. Theo Stillwater and Nestor Clayton, Etta's brother, were a matched pair, at least in height and breadth. Walking, massive, trees.

A grin split Theo's tanned face when he saw Gabe at the counter. "Hey, man, how's it shaking?"

"Good Theo. Sorry about your dad."

Theo's face sobered. "I can't believe the whole thing, First, he falls from his truck, and now someone attacks him in the hospital? What the hell is going on? I mean who would want to hurt my father? Thank heaven they put a guard on his room. Or I'd be camping beside his bed 24/7."

"Can you think of any reason someone would want to hurt your father?" Gabe asked. "Any run-ins he's had with people?"

Theo shook his head. "Nah. The old man hasn't mentioned anything like that. But you know, he's up there on his acreage, living his life the way he wants to, and I don't see that much of him. Or that's the way it was. Now this has happened, I realize I should try to spend more time with him. Something like this makes you realize how precious time is."

Etta brought a coffee over for Theo. "Speaking of run-ins, what about that fight over the water, Theo? Didn't I hear your dad was upset with his neighbor?"

Theo blew out a breath. "Yeah, but that's just two old guys arguing over whether the river that cuts through their land belongs to one or the other. Not something you'd want to kill a guy over."

"Tell me about the neighbor," Gabe said, pulling his notebook and pen out of his pocket.

"His name's Keith Stimmers. He and his wife have owned the property next to Dad forever. I like Keith even though he's sometimes an ornery cuss. But then, what old guy isn't?"

Gabe thought of The Viking, a geriatric prospector who had played a big role in helping Gabe solve the sabotage case last fall. It seemed ornery and old went together. But that didn't make the person unlikeable. Or a killer, for that matter.

"Your dad and Stimmers had a dispute over the river?"

Theo nodded and slurped his coffee. "Yeah. Dad says Keith built a dam on the river upstream, so the water flow to Dad's acreage is about a quarter of what it used to be. That makes it hard to grow anything and Dad makes a living off the vegetables he can take to the farmers' markets. So last I heard, Dad was going to sue Keith."

"What did Stimmers say to the threat? Did he know about it?"

Theo laughed. "Oh yeah, he knew. Dad said Keith told him he'd be wasting his money, and perhaps they should just have a fisticuff event. Sell tickets to townspeople. Make some money while they're bashing each other's heads in. I have to wonder who'd buy tickets to watch a couple of seventy-year-old scrawny men flail at each other."

Gabe got directions to the Stimmers' property from Theo and thanked Etta for the coffee and cookies. Before he left, he grabbed three more cookies. "For the road, it's a long one."

As he drove away from the resort, he waved at a young couple sitting in the sun on the front porch of one of the guest cabins. He'd checked out the rates a while ago when he had toyed with the idea of inviting Bethany to visit. Summer stays were priced at $150 a night. Not bad, when you were guaranteed unbelievable scenery, a swimming pool, trails and horses to ride on them, a bonfire every evening to go with your marshmallows. And Etta's gourmet meals if you didn't feel like cooking in your own cabin.

Bethany would undoubtedly have eaten in the main lodge. She wasn't big on cooking for one. Or even for two. When they'd been married, their meals together had been rare. She had her schedule with the network and was usually anchoring the news at dinnertime. He had his law practice and grabbed takeout on his way home. When they found a day that they could share a meal, it was something special, so they invariably went to a restaurant.

Last Thursday, the day they had received the divorce judgment, he and Bethany hadn't wanted to walk away from each other. Instead, and in keeping with their habit of marking special events with dinner, they had opted for dinner at a restaurant next to Le Germain, the hotel where he was staying.

After agreeing to meet Bethany at the restaurant at eight, Gabe had gone back to his hotel to change for dinner. He hadn't packed many clothes because this was to be a two-day trip, and a duty trip at that. He never needed a wide selection of clothes, especially living in Cheakamus, and a person didn't need variety to get divorced. Hell, jeans and a t-shirt would do it. Why dress up for the end of something you loved?

But he had thrown his favorite sweater into the duffel bag, and he hauled it out now. A gift from Bethany before things all went to hell. Cashmere, and a gray that she claimed made his blue eyes deepen with mystery. Sexy, she called it.

He pulled the sweater over his head and studied his image in the mirror. His eyes didn't look any different to him. But hey, if Beth saw something there, then he would wear the sweater.

When Bethany arrived at the restaurant, she looked exactly like the woman he remembered from their life on the ranch near Calgary. Free, fresh, and in love with the world. His heart skipped, and he stood as she approached. He hugged her and kissed her cheek. A sensation like the warm breeze in Grand Cayman caressed him.

They talked about everything and nothing. Her job, The Peak Bar, his latest investigation. When they exhausted the safe topics, Gabe reached his hand across the tabletop. "I miss you, babe. I will always love you. Even though we are now an old, divorced couple."

She smiled and touched his hand. "Not so old. And no one is saying we can't stay in touch and reconnect occasionally."

He lifted her hand and kissed it. "I love you, Beth. Staying in touch would be great."

She smiled like she had a secret and opened her handbag. Then she placed a small dark packet on the tabletop and pushed it toward him with a manicured finger. "Perhaps we could have a farewell tour?"

She nudged two more condom packets across the table. "Are you staying nearby?"

He stared at her.

She whispered. "By the way, did I tell you I love that sweater on you? It reminds me of everything wonderful we had."

Gabe noticed the server hovering nearby, a slight smile on

her lips. He turned to Bethany and said, "I'm staying at Le Germain, next door, if you really want that tour."

The server approached and cleared Gabe's plate. "Will you be wanting the check, sir?"

Bethany spit out laughter. "Oh yeah, we want the check."

Gabe grinned now as he remembered the farewell tour. He'd love it if they could imitate musicians and extend the farewell tour over a few years.

Then he shook his head. No point in daydreams. But this he knew: if, no—when, he found Drake's killer and cleared his own name, he and Bethany could begin again. She wouldn't be tainted by the stain of an accused murderer for a husband. He'd be vindicated, cleansed. And when they began again, he'd make sure they did more things together. Like grocery shopping and meal prep. Sunday dinners like Greta had. Sharing the little things in life and not just the big ones. Instinctively, he knew it was the little things that often mattered the most.

31

Tuesday, July 20, 2010
TIFFANY'S CAFÉ

GABE SAT in his booth at the back of Tiffany's, waiting on the dinner special. Tonight, it was beef stroganoff and noodles. That made three specials in a row which were not meatloaf. Another sign Rhonda had shaken off her depression.

He checked his notebook entries for the investigation: five pages so far, each one with a victim's name as the title.

Based on his call with Josie, he'd eliminated Patricia, the food bank treasurer, as a suspect in the death of the Wurtzes.

He'd also tentatively eliminated Charles Michelson, Lara's ex, as a suspect in her death. Charles had sent Gabe the information he promised. Gabe had checked with the hotels in Europe and verified that Charles had, in fact, been out of Canada during the weeks before Lara's death. All that remained was confirmation from Stan Wurtz that the company's financials looked legit.

"I know you aren't a forensic accountant," Gabe had said to Stan, "but you're an accountant and I'm not. Just tell me whether the business looks solid or if the numbers are hinky." Stan had agreed on the condition Gabe gave him sugar cube tossing lessons and then promised results by Saturday.

It was good to strike suspects from the list. But it would be even better to identify more suspects to add to his "who might the killer be" list. If these supposed accidents were related, Gabe needed a common thread between the victims. Ideally, he needed a suspect with a connection to more than one victim. He had nothing.

On the new leads side, Gabe had one in the Stillwater attack, and one in Lara's death.

The Stillwater lead came from his talk with Theo at Solomon's Choice. Keith Stimmers, the neighbor damming the river on Stillwater's land, could be a suspect.

As for the Lara lead, Gabe planned to talk to Kathaleen Quinn about Charles Michelson's revelation that Lara had threatened Kathaleen recently. According to Charles, the sisters may not have been as loving as Gabe thought.

So, he was down to a measly two leads. And neither of them seemed to connect to the other.

He picked up his phone and called his favorite Mountie, Sergeant LeBlanc, again. Once more, the call bounced to voicemail. "LeBlanc," Gabe said, "stop having the time of your life with my sister and call me back, will you? I have a gigantic puzzle I need your insights on. You should be celebrating. I mean, here I am asking for you to weigh in on a problem. Doesn't happen often, does it? Here's your chance to prove your superior detecting skills."

This was exactly the wrong time for LeBlanc to be off in Toronto. Corporal Lightheart was doing a piss-poor job managing the crime happening in Cheakamus while LeBlanc was away. If the RCMP moved LeBlanc to another detachment, and the residents of Cheakamus had to put up with Lightheart, the entire town was going to descend into mayhem.

Probably a good thing Harris and the town council had decided to set up their own police force.

Just then, Maxine entered Tiffany's and made her way to

the rack of coffee thermoses. She filled a mug, looked around the café, and spotted Gabe. He waved her over.

Maxine slid into the booth and grabbed the menu. "What's good tonight?"

"Rhonda's claiming to come from a long line of Russian chefs tonight. Beef stroganoff. Owen says it's excellent."

When Rhonda approached their booth, Maxine said, "Feed me. I'm starving." Then she leaned forward and lowered her voice. "And maybe when you bring my meal over, you can join us? I hear there might be news about the new police force."

"Hah. If Harris finds out I've been blabbing, he'll fire me from the council. Oh wait, then I'd be free of the position. I could use that time to go to a spa or to a therapist. Or take a vacation."

When Gabe and Maxine had finished their main course, Rhonda delivered three crème caramels to the booth and slid onto the seat beside Gabe. "My treat," she said. "I feel like I owe both of you because I've been crabby lately and I think I've taken it out on you more than once."

"Nah," Gabe said. "You've been your usual gay self, a veritable sunny presence in my otherwise dull life."

"Quit the bullshit, Gabrieli, or I'll ban you."

He raised his hands to signify surrender. "Okay. You were a tad testy last week. But we love you anyway."

"Better," Rhonda said. "Okay, so the police force." She pointed a finger at Maxine. "Off the record."

When Maxine mimicked zipping her lips, Rhonda said, "We approached LeBlanc, but he said he was considering leaving the Mounties and moving away. Some gobbledegook about career opportunities from afar that he couldn't allow to slip through his fingers."

Gabe jerked. "Moving away? Who am I going to annoy if he leaves?"

"I hope he doesn't move too far away," Rhonda said,

"because I know Lucy and he are a thing. Do you think she would leave Eau Claire and move wherever LeBlanc goes? Would that mean you'd have to go back there and manage her bar?"

Gabe shrugged. "She hasn't said one word to me. I don't plan to move back there, so she would probably hire a manager. Don't know, though, if she'd follow LeBlanc. Lucy isn't really the 'I will follow him' kinda gal."

Rhonda nodded. "That's what I think too. So, we have interviewed three candidates for the chief. My favorite is a seasoned officer from Alberta. I think Harris agrees with me, but I don't know about the others on the council."

"Alberta?" Gabe said. "That would be great. It's kinda lonely being the only Albertan here. A tough job too, trying to cram culture and rationality down everyone's throats. I could use the help."

32

Wednesday, July 21, 2010
THE STIMMERS' FARM

KEITH STIMMERS and his wife lived on sixty acres carved out of the birch and evergreens high on a hillside near Silverton Lake. Gabe's ears popped as he drove up the main road, looking for the side road that would take him to the farm. Theo had said, "Watch for Keith's sign nailed to a post on the north side of the road. It says, 'You are here.' You can't miss it."

Famous last words, "you can't miss it." Gabe hated to hear them. Invariably he spent most of the time wondering if he had missed whatever it was he couldn't miss.

This time, however, he noticed the sign immediately. You really couldn't miss it because it was about six feet by three feet. "You are here" had been painted on the sign in neon green and orange.

He turned onto the access road, really more of a single track through the bush. But someone, probably Keith, had laid down gravel to make it more than passable.

The road opened into a large clearing in front of a wide-fronted rancher. To the left of the clearing sat what appeared to be a machine shed and garage combo. He parked, exited the truck, and approached the front door of the house. As soon as he placed his foot on the steps leading to the porch, a dog barked from inside the house. A deep rumbling bark that made Gabe hesitate.

"Maudie, calm down," a woman said. The barking stopped.

Then a woman in her sixties, by Gabe's guess, opened the screen door and smiled at him. "Help you?"

Visions of the North Pole and elves popped into Gabe's head when the woman smiled at him. She was about the same age as Greta. However, Greta, with her spiky short hair and vibrant clothing, was more reminiscent of Judy Dench. The woman facing Gabe was Mrs. Claus.

A boxer pushed its nose past the woman's ample hips and issued another deep rumble. The woman tapped the boxer on its nose. "Maudie, you know better than to be rude." She turned to Gabe. "Sorry, she has absolutely no manners. I'm Martha Stimmers. What can I do for you?"

Gabe introduced himself and said he was hoping to talk to Keith. "It's about your neighbor Wilfred Stillwater."

The woman gasped and put a hand to her chest. "Oh my, I hope it's not bad news? I thought he was doing better?"

"Not bad news, no," Gabe said.

She smiled in relief. "That's good then. Keith is in the barn tending to some new piglets. Just follow the path behind the house."

The barn sat in a dip about a few hundred yards behind the house. The large doors were propped open and as Gabe approached, he could hear pigs squealing. He stepped inside the barn and took a minute to adjust his eyes to the dim interior. Theo had said that both Wilfred and Keith were "scrawny," but Gabe would have said "elf" if someone had asked him to describe Keith Stimmers.

The man standing inside the pigpen might have topped

five and a half feet in cowboy boots. But the rubber boots he wore today didn't give him as much of a lift. And his overalls looked to have been made for a man twice his size. Perhaps Keith was one of those men who added layers beneath his overalls in the winter, rather than invest in parkas. Right now, he cradled a squirming piglet with his left arm. He held a syringe in his right hand. "Hush, my beauty," he crooned. "Just one prick and you'll be all good. Won't hurt a bit."

The piglet released a string of high-pitched squeals and wriggled.

"Won't hurt a bit" was another of those phrases that meant the exact opposite. The piglet obviously wasn't born yesterday.

Gabe raised his voice to counter the squeals. "Mr. Stimmers?"

Keith jerked and turned to face Gabe. "Gave me a start there, son," he said. "I almost vaccinated myself."

"Apologies," Gabe said. "Your wife said I'd find you here."

"And you'd be?"

"Gabe Gabrieli, from Cheakamus. I wanted to talk to you about Wilfred Stillwater." He raised his hands quickly, and added, "Nothing dire. He's improved a bit, they say. I was hoping we could talk about the dispute you two had going on."

Keith turned to his side and spat a stream of brown juice onto the hay. "You mean the river?" When Gabe nodded, Keith said, "Tell you what. You help me get these little fellas vaccinated and I'm happy to talk to you."

Gabe climbed into the pigpen, careful to avoid stepping on any of the tiny bodies nosing around Keith's boots. "What do I do?"

Keith handed the piglet to Gabe. "One hand under her belly, the other under her chin. You hold 'em, I'll stick 'em. Mind they don't wriggle too hard because I'm likely to miss and get you instead."

Gabe clutched the piglet firmly. He hated needles. Almost as much as courtrooms and hospitals.

Keith glanced at Gabe. "You okay, son? You look kinda pale."

"Fine. Just don't poke me."

Keith chuckled. "Needle hater, eh? Can't blame you. Now, what can I tell you about the river?" He put his hand on the piglet's neck, spread the skin with his fingers, and inserted the needle. She jerked slightly, but didn't squeal.

Gabe put the piglet on the ground. "Story I heard is you blocked it upstream from Stillwater's place and cut off the flow for his vegetable garden. He was gonna sue you."

Keith pointed to the just-vaccinated piglet and said, "Put her on the other side of that barrier so we can keep track of which ones we've stuck." Gabe did so and then selected another piglet from the mass surrounding Keith.

"Right about his wanting to sue me," Keith said as he readied the syringe. "Wrong about blocking the river. Beavers did that." Keith hawked another glob of brown juice onto the hay before vaccinating the piglet in Gabe's arms.

They developed a rhythm. Pick up a piglet, ask a question, ready a syringe, stick the piglet, put that piglet across the barrier, spit tobacco juice onto the hay, answer the question. Repeat.

After the first two questions, Keith warmed up to the topic. "Nope," he said. "I didn't dam that river, but Willie didn't believe me. Even after I showed him the dam. I said we should work together to rip the dam apart, but no dice. He figured I'd built the dam so I could take it down."

"So, have you taken it apart?" Gabe asked.

Keith spat. "Not yet. I was so pissed at Willie that I figured he could wait a while longer for the river to be opened. He's not so innocent in all of this, let me tell you."

Gabe picked up the last piglet and cradled it. Its belly was warm in his hand. "How so?"

Keith readied the syringe. "He harvested trees from our land." Keith cracked a grin and waggled the syringe. "Actually, it was ingenious, but I won't tell him that. Martha and me, we spend winters in Mexico. It's just too frikkin cold here. So we go down there, and I hire teenagers from up the road to look after our animals. But last year we decided to have a family Christmas. All the kids came home, and we did it up right."

Keith laughed. "That's when we discovered Willie's side hustle." He put his hand on the piglet and gave the animal its shot. The little guy wriggled and let out a pitiful squeak.

Gabe cuddled the baby. "Shh, it's all done. You're good."

"They grow on ya, don't they?" Keith said. "Barely a week old and already learning life's not all rosy."

They climbed from the pigpen. "I'm done in here," Keith said. "Let's go back to the house."

As they walked up the hill toward the rancher, Keith said. "As I was saying, we noticed heavy traffic up the road past our turnoff and after watching it for about a week, I drove up for a look-see. Wouldn't you know, at the next turnoff, the one that takes you around the back of our property, there's a Christmas-tree shaped sign that says 'Willie's Trees. Cut your own. Cheap.'"

"He was selling your trees?" Gabe asked.

"You got it. When I showed up, there were at least a dozen vehicles parked along the road. People hauling Douglas firs out of the bush. *My* bush. Kids running through the woods, screeching and calling to their parents to come see this or that tree."

Keith stood still and put his hands on his hips, grinning. "*And.* Willie had a firepit there, complete with logs to sit on. And a trailer where people could buy hot cider or coffee. And weenies or marshmallows."

Gabe chuckled. "Entrepreneurial."

"You got that right. Willie claimed he thought the trees were on provincial land. Well, that's a bunch of hooey because back in the day he helped me fence the back few acres. 'Oh yeah,' he says when I reminded him of that, 'guess my mind's slipped a bit as I've aged.' How long you been selling my trees, I asked him. And he said, 'few years, maybe six. But I wasn't selling your trees. I was selling government trees. Or so I thought.'"

Keith started along the path again. "And then the beavers come along and dam up our river. Do you believe in karma, Gabe?"

"Not really." Gabe filed Keith's question under "Clue, possible."

Keith shook his head. "Me neither. What you haven't asked me yet is whether I clobbered Willie and put him in that coma."

"Did you?"

"Nope. Sure, we had our petty squabbles, but he's a good neighbor even though he owes me a few dozen trees. Nope, Martha and I were in Toronto when Willie ended up in hospital. We went to meet our newest grandson. Not much bigger than those piggies we vaccinated back there. But more cuddly and not as squawky."

"I hate to sound like a cop…," Gabe said.

"But can I prove it?" Keith said. "You can check Martha's Facebook page for about three thousand pictures of the little guy. Or I can give you names of people who can confirm we were there."

"Names would be good," Gabe said. He pulled his card from his wallet and handed it to Keith. "Just email me the names. And thanks for letting me hold the piglets."

"Any time, son. They'll be due for a booster in two weeks. I'll be calling."

Keith turned toward the front of his house, and Gabe

climbed into his truck. Before he could press the ignition, Keith swerved around and waved. Gabe lowered his window.

Keith approached the truck and rested his hands on the window frame. "There's one thing. Could mean something. Could be nothing."

33

Wednesday, July 21, 2010
THE PEAK BAR

WHEN GABE ENTERED The Peak Bar later Wednesday afternoon, Harris and John Smith were standing behind the bar, eyeing an off-kilter row of Irish coffee glasses. "I think there's something he does with his wrist," Harris said.

Smitty flexed his right wrist. "Here goes." He held a sugar cube level with his eye, moved his arm back and forth as if he was about to fling a dart at the dartboard, and then lobbed the sugar cube toward the line of glasses. It tumbled through the air and plopped into the bar sink short of the first glass. "Well, heck."

A patron sitting on a barstool near the end of the row of glasses laughed out loud. "John, my boy, I think we should change the pool. Instead of 'when will Gabe miss,' it would be 'when will Smitty sink one?' If 'never' is a choice in the pool, I'm in. It's a sure thing."

"You ever try it?" Smitty asked. "It ain't easy."

"Sure it is," Gabe said, approaching the bar. "All it takes is a little practice. And about a thousand sugar cubes." He grabbed an apron and pulled the strap over his head before he grabbed three sugar cubes from the box. "Watch carefully."

Gabe rolled his shoulders, flexed his hips, scuffed at the

floor like a pitcher on his mound. Then he tossed the cubes in rapid succession. Ping, ping, ping. Three sinkers. "That's all there is to it."

"Maybe I'm not flexing my hips enough?" Smitty asked.

Harris shrugged. "Don't quit your day job. You're not ready for the cube tossing circuit."

A young fellow rose from his table under the windows on the far side of the barroom and approached the bar, pulling his headphones away from his head and catching them in his long hair.

He grinned at Gabe and held out his hand. "Hey man, how're ya doing? When you were out at the lake, I thought you looked familiar, and now I know why. You're that sugar-cube pitching bartender, right? Yeah, you are."

Gabe stared at him and then shook his hand. "That's me. And you are…"

"Connor. Connor Johnson, from the sailboat rentals?"

The light dawned. Surfer dude. "Of course, Connor! You look different without a paintbrush in your hand. Still listening to horror books?"

"Only if I'm sure no one's gonna sneak up behind me."

Connor turned to Harris and Smitty. "Hiya."

Gabe did the honors. "This is Harris Chilton, my partner. And John Smith, who works with us."

"John Smith?" Connor said. "Seriously?"

Gabe grinned. "Yep, that's exactly what I said when Smitty applied for a job here. Told him it was a good thing he wasn't trying to rent a hotel room because I'd never give him the key." Gabe turned to the others. "Connor works out at Silverton Lake. He's the guy who discovered Lara Quinn's body the other day."

Smitty said, "Man, that must have been awful."

Connor shuddered. "It was grim. I tried to save her, you know? CPR and stuff? But it was useless." He stared into the distance and then shuddered again. "I really don't want to experience that again. I feel like I failed her."

"You did what you could, buddy," Gabe said. "Sometimes it's just too late."

———

Later, when no customers were within earshot, Smitty whispered to Gabe, "I'm pretty sure I saw her in town before that day. That lady who died."

Gabe said, "Really? When was this?"

Smitty stared at the ceiling and scratched his head. "Dunno. Musta been when you were in Calgary. But like, maybe it wasn't even her. Maybe it was another woman named Lara."

"How do you know her name was Lara?" Gabe asked.

"Because I saw her outside the Red Dragon and the woman she was with shouted it at her."

"Shouted? They were arguing? Did you hear anything?"

"Bits and pieces. The one called Lara said, 'Stop trying to run my life. It's my money.' And then later she said, 'Keep interfering and maybe I'll give it all to him. Cut you out completely.'" Smitty shrugged. "That's about it. They noticed me standing nearby and shot me some nasty looks, so I beat it."

"Did you get the name of the other woman?"

Smitty studied the ceiling some more. "I dunno if it was her name, because it didn't make sense to me. At one point, the Lara woman said, 'Stop it kaycue.' I think maybe she was saying 'okay' and got it garbled up."

Kaycue. Huh. "Tell me what she looked like," Gabe said.

Smitty closed his eyes and pursed his lips. "Middle aged, maybe older? Over fifty for sure. Short hair. Going gray in places. Pretty fit for an old woman. I remember she kept messing with her earring. Turning it with her fingers. It was a pearl, I think."

As Smitty described the woman, a picture formed in Gabe's mind. A woman playing with her pearl earring. Not kaycue. But K.Q. Kathaleen Quinn's initials.

Smitty's version of the sisters' spat sounded similar to what Charles Michelson had told Gabe during their phone conversation. That Lara had threatened to change her will, cutting Judge Quinn out of a sizeable inheritance.

34

Wednesday, July 21, 2010
CHEAKAMUS MEDICAL CLINIC

THE WAITING room at the medical clinic was almost as noisy as the construction going on above Tiffany's Café. Rhonda had hoped that she'd be able to close her eyes and zone out while she waited for her follow-up appointment with Dr. Chickle. But no.

Back at the café, workmen were renovating the upper floor of the building, getting it ready for Rhonda's new tenant. Cheryl had worked wonders leasing out the space—three days was all it took, and Rhonda had five proposals from prospective business tenants. Selecting the winner was easy. It was a proposal that meshed well with Rhonda's secret desire. Plus, the tenant was someone Rhonda knew and trusted.

She offered the workmen free meals if they shut down the noisiest part of the renovation during the breakfast, lunch, and dinner rushes in the café. That way, her diners could enjoy their meals without wearing noise-canceling earphones.

They were only two days into the makeover, and already Rhonda was dreaming about hammers and skill saws in her sleep. Her body vibrated in tune with the noise from overhead.

And now, in the waiting room, Rhonda discovered that

babies and toddlers were noisier than hammers. She'd forgotten that fact in the years since Roxanne and David had been toddlers.

Over in the corner, a set of twins screeched and fought over who could play with the building blocks. Across the room, a colicky baby wailed in its agony. And next to Rhonda, a cherubic nine-month-old gurgled and chuckled at her while trying to crawl into her lap.

"Sorry," the young mother said to Rhonda, "Lola's at that age where she wants to explore any and all laps."

Rhonda gazed at the cheerful baby and remembered Roxy at that age. Just as roly-poly, just as quick to grin at anyone who engaged with her. Just as cuddly.

"Hello Lola," Rhonda said. "You remind me of my daughter fifteen years ago."

Lola gurgled and waved her fists in the air. Then she pushed away from her mother's arms and touched Rhonda's face with a tiny, slobber-covered hand. "Oh lord," the mom said. "She also delights in sucking on her hand."

Rhonda laughed and put her hands out to Lola, who immediately crawled onto her lap. Settled there and grinned at her mom. The baby warmed Rhonda's lap. "She's a love," Rhonda said.

"Today," the mom said. "Today she's being a darling because she's in public. It's only at home that the demon side comes out." The mom chucked Lola beneath her chin and giggled. "Isn't that right, sweetie? You save all your growing pains for your mother."

Rhonda rocked the baby. "I remember those days so well. Thankfully, my kids are grown and close to leaving the nest." As she said that, Rhonda's heart sank. It was true. Soon David would be off to university. And Roxy would probably follow in a year, unless she made good on her vow to hike around Europe or try out for the Olympic gymnastics team.

Rhonda and Frank would be empty nesters. And if Cheryl

found a buyer for the café, Rhonda would be a woman with nothing to do. Except lie around watching daytime TV. Maybe she could get involved in provincial politics.

She scolded herself. Give your head a shake, woman. First things first. She'd visited Dr. Chickle two days ago and now the doctor wanted to run one more test. "Nothing to worry about," the doctor had said.

But what person didn't worry when a doctor said they wanted to run a new test? Rhonda had a sense of dread about the whole situation. If only Frank was here instead of out on the highway with an eighteen-wheeler.

"Rhonda?" the receptionist said. "Follow me."

Rhonda gave Lola a quick cuddle and handed her back to her mother. "Nice meeting you Lola. You brightened my day." Then she followed the receptionist down the hall and entered an examination room.

———

FIFTEEN MINUTES LATER, Rhonda stood on the sidewalk outside the clinic, wondering how she got there. The sun was still blazing down on Main Street, the squirrels were still chasing each other around the trunk of the birch tree near the curb, the traffic light at the corner still blinked green, yellow, red. Nothing had changed.

Yet, everything had changed.

Rhonda walked to a bench outside the pharmacy next door and sat. Then she phoned Frank.

When he answered, she said, "You need to come home, lover. I've just come from the doctor's. It's serious. I need you here."

35

Thursday, July 22, 2010
JUDGE QUINN'S HOUSE, NEAR CHEAKAMUS

BEFORE GABE HAD LEFT The Peak Bar Wednesday evening, Kathaleen Quinn had phoned him.

"My clerk says you'd like to meet. I have time tomorrow afternoon, if you want to come to the Courthouse. We can meet in my chambers."

Gabe had grimaced. Courthouses topped his list of things to be avoided. "Uhhh. What's the second option?"

Quinn hesitated and then said, "My home? It's close to Cheakamus."

When Gabe agreed, she gave him the address and told him to show up around three the next day.

Now, he sat in his truck outside a two-story house in an oval clearing amongst the evergreens just off Stockman's Road. He speculated that her property line edged the west side of Seamus O'Malley's ranch, the site of Gabe's recent steer-wrestling debacle.

Not long after he arrived, a gray Subaru roared down the driveway toward him, dust spiraling behind it. He recognized Quinn at the wheel. She slowed and stopped beside his truck, then threw open her door and climbed out. "Sorry, sorry.

Hope you haven't been waiting long. I got held up with the last case of the day."

She grabbed her briefcase from the car. "Shall we?"

She opened the front door and waved him inside the house. Gabe stepped in to a sunlit foyer that gave way to an open space, separated by a counter into a living section and kitchen area. Pulled up to the counter were six bar stools. Wood beams and trimmings gave the house a warm, welcoming air.

Stairs led up to what Gabe assumed would be the bedrooms. Through a set of glass French doors off the kitchen, he could see a den that appeared to have a view of the trees at the rear of the property.

"I'll make some coffee," Quinn said. "Decaf or full test?"

Internally, Gabe grimaced at the thought of decaf coffee. "Either is fine," he said, while silently begging the Head Honcho to tilt the odds in his favor.

"Full test it is then," Quinn said. "Frankly, I drink decaf only under duress."

He knew there was something he liked about this woman.

While the judge attended to the coffeemaker, Gabe plunked himself on a stool at the counter. As soon as he did so, a blue-eyed, long-haired cat leaped onto the countertop and chirped. Its coat was a mix of beige and white, and its tail was a dark brown duster. Its white face formed a heart beneath the brown of its ears and forehead. A Siamese whose hair was on steroids was as close as Gabe could come to identifying it.

Not sure whether the animal was allowed on the counter, Gabe sat still, afraid to encourage the cat to stick around. The cat chirped again and padded along the counter toward Gabe. Two feet away, it suddenly flung itself onto its side and offered its tummy for a rub. Quinn glanced around from the coffeemaker. "Diva! Stop being so promiscuous!"

The cat rolled over and gazed at the Judge. Then she rolled back toward Gabe and chirped.

"Pet her at your peril," Quinn said. "She will cleave herself to you for the entire time you are here if you show her any affection. She's basically a ham. Wants you to think she's love starved. Also, that I don't feed her."

Gabe wondered if Diva liked chicken, or had the same opinion as Doofus. "What breed is she?"

"A rag doll. Very placid, yet very demanding. And the reason there are no carpets in this house."

After she poured their coffees, the judge led Gabe into the den. Floor to ceiling windows framed the view of the evergreens and garden at the back of the house. He spotted well-tended veggie boxes and a row of birdhouses on tall stakes guarding the raspberry patch.

Gabe tasted the coffee. "Mmmm, good. Oso Negro beans?"

"Correct. The same beans as Rhonda uses at Tiffany's. In fact, that's where I first tasted this Raleigh Blend."

Gabe set his cup down on a side table and opened his small black notebook. He extracted a pen from his jacket pocket and clicked it open. "I spoke with Lara's ex, and I have someone looking into the company finances. However, his alibi checks out. Is there anything else about Lara or her life I should know? Any troubles she might have mentioned? Conflicts with neighbors? Stalkers?"

The judge sipped her coffee and after a moment said, "Before Lara and Charles set up their own business, a few years ago, there was a situation at Lara's day job with a superior who was verbally abusive. Lara reported the woman to HR and there was an internal investigation. When they fired the woman, she threatened to get even with Lara."

"Where is this woman now?"

"It happened ages ago. I heard she was in the U.S., somewhere on the east coast."

"Had Lara seen her since? Or received any communications?"

Quinn shrugged. "Don't know."

"Tell me the woman's name and the company."

After he jotted down Quinn's information, Gabe closed his notebook and stashed it and the pen in his pocket. "How did you and Lara get along? See each other often?"

"Not that often. This trip to visit me was the first time we'd been together since Christmas. She was busy. So was I. You know how it is."

"But you were close?"

Quinn shot him an inquisitive look. "Yes, we were. Why the twenty questions?"

"I heard that you might have had an argument with her the other day."

Her mouth opened. Then closed. She sputtered. "What?" Then she laughed. "Well, someone might be stirring things up. I sure can't remember an argument between us."

He shouldn't have been surprised at the lie. Didn't he know most everyone lied? Cops. Witnesses. Lawyers. But he had warmed to Judge Quinn and had filed her in the same category as LeBlanc and Rhonda: shooters, straight.

Gabe hated it when he misfiled people.

36

Thursday, July 22, 2010

ROCQUE & HOUND GUEST HOUSE

ON THURSDAY, around dinnertime, Greta phoned Gabe at The Peak Bar. "Gabe, can you come by the house? Anders is here and wants to talk to you."

Anders Thorvaldsen was a reclusive prospector who mostly roared around the nearby mountains on his ATV. The local kids called him The Viking and Gabe had to admit that Anders possessed the spirit, if not the build, of the breed. He'd been crucial in Gabe's investigation of the sabotage case, spotting one of the saboteurs stashing a truck in the bush.

Gabe had seen little of The Viking since that case and missed the old guy. But taking the time to go to Greta's now would interfere with the task he had to finish at the bar today. "I'm in the middle of taking inventory, Greta. Tell Anders to come to the bar."

"I've just put minestrone on the stove and have promised Anders homemade bread to go with it."

Gabe's mouth watered. "How big a pot of soup do you have there?"

Greta chuckled. "When have you known me to make less than a full stockpot?"

"Five minutes. Don't start without me."

Gabe shucked his apron, pocketed his phone and jumped into his truck. He eased to a stop outside the Rocque & Hound Guesthouse a mere three minutes and twenty seconds after Greta's call. Really, seeing as Greta's house was a short two blocks up the hill from the Bar, one could say Gabe had dawdled on his way.

Hound greeted Gabe when he entered the house, prancing back and forth and nosing Gabe's boots as he tried to remove them. "Don't even think about chewing on these boots, Hound. I'll have to report you to Greta if you do. And you know how she gets when you're naughty."

The Viking sat in his usual seat at Greta's kitchen table with a steaming mug of tea in front of him. His gnarled fingers cradled the mug as if seeking warmth to ease their aches. He looked up as Gabe entered the room and grinned. His piercing, brilliant blue eyes never failed to astonish Gabe. As usual, The Viking's fine white hair stuck out at several angles around his head. If he didn't get a trim soon, he'd have to braid it. Of course, it would be a sorry, skimpy braid. Sort of like Anders himself. No one could ever call Anders rotund. Or even pudgy. Or average. This Viking was a pipsqueak. Maybe an inch taller than the other pipsqueak Gabe had recently talked to—Keith Stimmers.

The Viking pushed himself upright and stuck his hand out toward Gabe. "Sonny, how ya doin'? Still chasing bad guys in your spare time, I hear."

Gabe shook Anders' hand and pulled out a chair from the table. He eased himself onto the chair, moaning softly as his knee protested.

"Hurt yourself, sonny?"

Gabe rubbed his knee. "It's almost better."

Greta brought three bowls of minestrone to the table, along with a loaf of bread. "Why don't you slice the bread,

Gabe?" she said. After she sat at the table, she said to Anders, "Gabe dinged up his knee playing cowboy out at O'Malley's ranch. Steer wrestling, no less."

"Oh, yeah?" The Viking said. "What was your best time, sonny?"

Gabe thought for a second. "Best time for missing the steer completely, four seconds. Best time for being dragged around the arena by a steer who didn't play by the rules, eighteen seconds."

"Hah! Funny how those animals don't just lie down and quit when you grab them by the horns." The Viking dipped a slice of bread into his soup. "I hear you're looking into what happened to Willie Stillwater."

"I am. Where did you hear that?"

"Keith Stimmers."

Gabe stopped spooning his soup. "Ahh. You're the person who Keith said might have some information for me? Who saw something that might be nothing?"

The Viking nodded.

"Keith wouldn't tell me your name," Gabe said. "He said he knew someone who might help but didn't want to 'blow his cover,' as if you were under a witness protection program."

"Yeah, that's Keith. Course, he don't know that you and I go back a way. Or that I helped you with that sabotage case. Or that I taught you all about prospecting."

"You know Wilfred Stillwater?" Gabe asked.

The Viking nodded and slurped up some soup. "Mmmm, Greta, you outdid yourself this time. Just the right kick. Yep. Willie and Keith and I are old buddies. Went to grade school together. Called ourselves the Three Musketeers and fought off all the big bullies. 'Cause the three of us together didn't probably weigh as much as a baby St. Bernard."

The three of them as adults probably didn't weigh as much as an adult St. Bernard. Not much had changed in sixty-odd years.

Grabbing another slice of bread, Anders said, "I was tooling around the flats by the highway the night that Willie got himself hurt. I saw his truck go by. Heading west. And he had someone in the truck with him. Didn't think much of it at the time."

"Who was with him?" Gabe asked.

The Viking shook his head and shrugged. "Dunno. Had a bush hat on. Young, is my guess. A guy, I think. He was leaning against the passenger door, turned toward Willie so I couldn't see his face. It was dark out, and Willie was booting it along the road."

"Huh. Okay, thanks."

"Interesting isn't it how I find your bad guys for you, eh sonny?"

Gabe nodded. "Trucks and the people in them, that's your superpower, Anders."

"Well, that and a few hundred other things, mebbe." The Viking glanced across the table at Greta. "Any chance of a refill?" He pushed his empty soup bowl forward.

Gabe pushed his bowl forward, too.

"What do you know about the argument Wilfred and Keith were having over the river?" Gabe asked The Viking.

"You mean the beaver dam?" The Viking chuckled. "Willie told me he knew all along it was beavers that built it. But he'd never admit it to Keith."

"Do you think Keith could have attacked Wilfred?"

The Viking's spoon stopped halfway to his open mouth. "I heard the guy who attacked Willie in the hospital could run like a track star. You've met Keith. How do you think he'd do in a footrace?" Anders shook his head and slurped some soup. "You oughta stay out of the sun. It's affecting your head, sonny."

The Viking had a point. Keith was a very unlikely suspect. Not just from his size and age, but also because Gabe had called the people who were with the Stimmers in Ontario last week. Everyone confirmed Keith had been where he said he'd been.

Of course, Keith could have hired someone to attack Wilfred Stillwater. But Gabe couldn't believe Santa's head elf knew any hitmen.

37

Friday, July 23, 2010

JUDGE QUINN'S HOUSE

Early Friday morning, as he drove along Stockman's Road toward Judge Quinn's turnoff, Gabe recalled the looks on the faces of the women when he entered Tiffany's at six o'clock. Maxine, Etta, and Rhonda had been standing in a tight clump near the muffin display. They were laughing when he entered, but when Rhonda spotted him, she choked off her laugh and shouted. "Oh hi, Gabe. You're up early."

Shouting as if he was standing half a block away, instead of a mere five feet. And the minute Rhonda greeted him, Maxine and Etta's faces morphed into pictures of...what? On a five-year-old, it would have been a look of "we've been naughty."

And Rhonda had actually blushed.

He talked to his truck as he turned onto Judge Quinn's access road. "What do you think they were up to, Three?" Silence from the truck.

"And why did they all get the giggles when I asked which of the morning coffees was fresh and hot?"

When he stopped in front of Judge Quinn's front door, Gabe turned off the engine, patted the dash, and said, "You think on that mystery, Three, while I go try to solve the mystery of two sisters. Sounds like something from Agatha Christie, eh?"

His phone pinged as he walked down the path to Judge Quinn's front door. A text from Jack:

> "Change of plans tomorrow. Going hiking with Roxy up at Prim's Folly. Raincheck?"

Gabe responded with a thumbs up and then pressed Judge Quinn's doorbell.

It would have been great to spend some time with his kid brother, but Gabe was a realist. No way an older brother could compete with a high school heartthrob. And without a doubt, Jacko's heart throbbed mightily where Roxy Zalesko was concerned. Roxy checked all the boxes on Gabe's list of "who's good for my baby brother." Honest. Check. Animal lover. Check. Sense of humor. Check. Independent. Check. Keeps Jack on straight and narrow. Definite check.

When Judge Quinn answered the door, she hugged her thick terry robe to her waist. Her face showed she was not pleased with her doorbell chiming before seven in the morning.

"Did we have an appointment?" she said.

Gabe held out a tray holding the coffees and muffins he'd bought at Tiffany's. "I don't know about you, but I'm a total bear before my morning coffee."

Judge Quinn stared at him. Diva, the ragdoll cat, appeared by her side and then wove her body around Gabe's ankles. She rubbed her head on his jeans, purring loudly.

The judge sighed and held the door open. "I suppose because you are Diva's new best friend, I have to let you in."

Gabe would have to bring the cat a treat next time. Maybe a dozen of the tins of chicken-flavored cat food he had in his suite.

"Sorry it's so early," he said as he followed the judge down her hallway. "But I wanted to catch you before you left for work. Won't take long."

The judge peeked inside the bag of muffins and extracted one. Then she reached for a coffee, but hesitated.

Gabe pointed to the coffee on her left. "Raleigh Blend."

She nodded her thanks. "I can give you five minutes. Starting now."

The judge obviously hadn't yet had her morning coffee.

Gabe popped a piece of blueberry muffin into his mouth and pulled his cell phone from his pocket. "I want you to listen to a voicemail. Charles Michelson replayed it for me last night and I recorded it."

When he placed his phone on the countertop, the judge moved closer. Gabe pressed the play button on the recording.

"Hi Charles, it's me. Just a heads up. I told KQ we were talking about reducing the royalty or even getting rid of it. She went ballistic. Said I should be committed to a facility for the insane. Long story short, I lost it too and threatened to cut her out of my will if she didn't stop trying to run my life. If she calls you in a snit, now you know why. Call me."

Gabe had watched color creep up the judge's face as she listened to the recording. Now, he clicked the stop button. "That's your sister, correct?"

The judge nodded and sighed. "Okay, I fibbed. We did argue. She said the divorce made her look at things differently, and she didn't hate Charles, so why make his life difficult? She planned to cut the royalty in half. I objected."

"That's putting it mildly, if Lara's words are true."

"Yes. It got a bit heated. But later, over dinner, we patched things up. I agreed that her life was hers to live."

Gabe asked, "Why did you lie?"

Judge Quinn shook her head. "It wasn't relevant. It had nothing to do with her death."

He stared at her silently.

The judge said, "I know. Stupid. I thought knowing we had argued would distract you. But…"

"But it made me chase around to determine whether you were hiding something vital. And now I am left wondering what else you aren't telling me."

Quinn hugged herself. "That's it. There's nothing more to tell. Except that I don't care about the inheritance. I'd give it all up to have Lara back. And more."

38

Friday, July 23, 2010
PRIM'S FOLLY, NEAR CHEAKAMUS

THE HELPER WAS WORKING this morning. Not at his paying job, however. Instead, he was working to right wrongs.

It was a perfect time to wander around the Folly mine site and work out a plan. Although this day promised to be hot, as usual for late July in the southern British Columbia mountains, the morning sun was comfortably warm, and a soft breeze made the wildflowers nod their heads as he strolled through them.

Prim's Folly, the abandoned tungsten mine site, had mostly been reclaimed by nature. All that remained of the old workings was the skeleton of a headframe, which was slowly graying. Headframes were outdoor elevators, consisting of a sturdy tower, topped by sheave wheel or pulley, and a system of cables and buckets for lowering workers and supplies down the mine shaft to the tunnels, and for hauling ore to the surface. Someone had removed the sheave wheel and cables from the Folly's headframe.

He'd heard the Folly used to be owned by Greta Rocque's father, Silas Jones. The rumor was that old Silas committed suicide by jumping off a ledge on Rimrock Mountain after his partner cheated him in a business deal involving the Folly.

Who knew if the rumor was true? What The Helper did know was that this old headframe stood over top of a deep shaft. The lower seven feet or so of the structure (what The Helper thought of as the tower's legs) were surrounded by wood planks, turning the structure into a roofless shed with a wooden elevator rising from its interior. A padlocked wooden door allowed access to the interior of shed.

The Helper dropped his backpack to the ground. He unzipped it and extracted a short crowbar. He placed the claw end of the bar between the lock's hasp and the door and pulled back. The ancient wood splintered quickly, and the hasp and lock detached from the door.

When he pulled the door open it sagged on its hinges and the bottom edge grated along the dirt. He removed a flashlight from his pack and shone it inside the space beyond the door.

The corners of the space were occupied by the four legs of the headframe tower. Centered between the legs was the mine shaft. The entire enclosure was perhaps eight- or ten-feet square.

A metal lid covered the mine shaft opening. The Helper presumed that was to prevent idiots falling to their death. When he inspected the lid, he saw it was secured on two sides with hasps and padlocks. Five more minutes with the crowbar, a fair bit of muscle and sweat, and he'd broken both hasps away from the lid.

He lifted the lid, and shoved it back from the opening, just far enough to allow him to shine the flashlight at the opening to see what lay below. A narrow wooden ladder affixed to one side of the shaft descended into the dark depths. The flashlight beam wasn't strong enough for him to see where the bottom of the shaft was. But this was a mine, so he guessed it had to be forty feet or more.

The shaft itself was about four feet a side. Wide enough that a person who wasn't paying attention could easily fall and not catch themselves.

Perfect.

The Helper pulled the lid back over the opening, grabbed his flashlight and crowbar, and exited the shed, pushing its door closed behind him.

Things had reached a crisis point. Old man Stillwater was still alive. The Helper's one chance to correct his original mistakes when he first tried to kill Stillwater in the casino parking lot had gone all wrong. It had started out smooth as silk. He'd crept up the stairs in the hospital and when he got to the second floor, he'd peeked through the stairwell doorway. No one at the nurse station. He could hear women's voices coming from one of the rooms however, so he knew the nurses were close by.

He tiptoed along the hall until he came to the first of the rooms with a window facing the hallway. Empty. The nurses' voices were closer now. Geez, were they in Stillwater's room? That would be a drag.

He crept further along the hall and glanced into the second windowed room. And there was Stillwater, out cold, alone.

The Helper rushed into the room. Wrote his message on the white board. Then it all started to go south. He unplugged all the machines in the room and ripped the IV out of Stillwater's arm. He'd been sure cutting off the IV would kill Stillwater outright. But no. So, he'd placed the pillow over the old guy's face and pressed down. But then the bells started ringing. Who knew there were alarms on those stupid machines?

It only took a second to realize the bells meant trouble, so he blasted his way out of Stillwater's room, down the hall and into the stairway. He heard the nurses shouting at him as the door closed behind him. He figured he'd got away with a second to spare. Pretty sure no one saw his face.

But now he'd heard things were looking up for Stillwater and that he might regain consciousness soon. And they had a friggin cop guarding his room. That meant no joy trying to get in there and finish the job.

And if the old guy came to, he'd be able to tell everyone who had been in his truck with him that night at the casino lot. Not good. No. Definitely not good.

Which meant he had to finish things now. Tomorrow at the latest. So that when Stillwater woke up, The Helper would be done with his tasks. Most of them. And he would be gone. Long gone. Karma wasn't perfect, but Mom always said you couldn't expect perfection.

He turned his face to the sun and smiled as it warmed his face. It was going to be a good day tomorrow.

39

Friday, July 23, 2010
TIFFANY'S CAFÉ

RHONDA HUMMED to herself as she sat on a stool at the counter in Tiffany's, enjoying a mug of coffee and a moment of quiet. She thought back to this morning when Gabe had walked in looking for takeout coffees. The memory gave her the giggles all over again.

Etta had just delivered the day's muffins, and Maxine had come for coffee.

"So," Maxine had said. "My receptionist is intent on meddling in my love life. 'I think that bartender slash detective is hot for you,' Josephine told me yesterday. I assured her he was not."

"Not hot for you?" Etta said. "Or not hot?"

"The former," Maxine said.

"I'll tell you a story," Rhonda said. "When Gabe and his truck first appeared in town last October, he parked in front of the café. Naturally, he came in here looking for breakfast. I was running the front counter that day and waited on him. 'Welcome to Tiffany's,' I said, 'famous for more than breakfast.' He looked up from the menu and I spotted a band-aid on his forehead above the remnants of a shiner. And I thought 'uh-oh, trouble here.' And then he quirked up his lip on the right side in that way he does when he's a bit amused and said, 'Are you Tiffany?' And his voice was, you know, husky. Honest to god, ladies, my heart went pitty-pat. I figured maybe it was merely early morning raspiness, but still it hit me like a lightning bolt, and I stammered around and said something about not looking like a Tiffany. And he nodded, slow-like and stared at me for a moment."

Rhonda paused and fanned her face. "And then he said, 'D. S. Gabrieli. But call me Gabe. Everyone does.' And his voice the second time was just as husky and I thought, 'Oh, sweet Jesus, definite trouble here.' I swear when he spoke to me in the café that day, a vision of rumpled bedding appeared in my head."

Rhonda smiled. "When Gabe is feeling relaxed and at ease with the world, I could listen to him talk all day long. And his eyes. Even with that shiner, his eyes made me warm and mushy inside. I know I'm older than he is, but hey, when the hormones get stirred up, they get stirred up. They don't pay any attention at all to who's done the stirring. So, first chance I got, I phoned Frank and told him to get his ass back to town, pronto."

Rhonda laughed. "As I was saying, Gabe is ..." She inhaled, paused, then breathed the word, "Hhhhhot."

Maxine grinned. "Does your husband know how you feel about Gabe?"

"I think he suspects," Rhonda said. "Now and then he suggests we go to The Peak for a nightcap. It's always on a night Gabe's working and Frank always grabs a couple of stools at the bar. And he never speaks to Gabe first, always waits for Gabe to say, 'Hey, how're you doing? What can I get for you?' And of course, about then I start thinking—"

"What are you offering?" Maxine interjected, grinning.

"Yeah, exactly. The upshot is Frank and I never stay long, and we always have a hot time in the hay that night. Without fail. So, yeah, I think he suspects."

The three of them were in the midst of gleeful laughter when Gabe walked into the café. Rhonda raised her voice so her friends wouldn't say anything he shouldn't hear. "Oh, hi, Gabe. You're up early."

He backed a step away and studied their faces. Then he had glanced at the rack of coffee thermoses. "Hey Rhonda. What's fresh and hot this morning?"

At which point, the three of them had collapsed into giggles, like a bunch of teenagers.

Poor Gabe. He'd bought his muffins and coffees and beat it out of the café faster than a calf running from a branding iron. She'd have to think up some story to feed him if he asked her what they had been laughing about.

Meanwhile, she needed to plan tonight's special. No need for meatloaf, now that Frank was home. He had driven straight home after she had called him from the doctor's office. Broke all the rules about trucker safety. It was ten at night when he walked into their house. They had talked about the situation for an hour and then went to bed. For the first time in a month, Rhonda slept through the night. Just having Frank with her calmed her and kept the fears away.

The next day, they had talked some more. Made a plan to deal with what was a life-altering diagnosis. Not fatal, thank heaven. But definitely enough to tilt Rhonda's world.

They agreed Rhonda would sell the café, as she planned. Relax and focus on her health. Frank would hire another driver for the long-haul routes and would do trips that didn't keep him away from home for more than a day. When the time was right, they would tell David and Roxy. Explain to them that the new reality wouldn't interfere with their plans for their future. Calm their fears.

Cheryl MacMillan, her realtor and friend, entered Tiffany's then, breaking the spell. Rhonda drained her coffee and rose from her stool.

"Is he here yet?" Cheryl asked. Yesterday Cheryl had told

Rhonda that Sergei Kravachenko, a short-order cook and diner owner from High River, Alberta, was driving to Cheakamus and wanted to check out Tiffany's.

Rhonda waved at the almost empty café. "No."

Cheryl checked her phone for messages. "I'm sure it won't be long. Last night I spoke to a friend who lives in High River. She told me Sergei's food is sublime."

Cheryl stashed her phone at the same time as the café door opened, and a burly man entered. "Hi, I'm Sergei," he said.

Rhonda took one look at him and knew in her heart he was a diner owner. And a successful one. The several extra pounds around the midsection were a sign the man loved his food. Brown eyes that stared into your soul. Mostly white hair, pulled back in a thick braid that hung at least six inches down his back. A neatly trimmed beard. Did he play Santa in High River for the little kids?

After Cheryl did the introductions, Sergei stood still and looked around the café. "Oof," he said. "This is a place people love to hang out, eh? You can feel the hug it wants to give you."

Rhonda had never thought of Tiffany's as a hug. Tiffany's was a come-as-you-are party, leave your attitude at the door, share your worries, celebrate successes, slap a neighbor on the back, tell a joke, sit by yourself and contemplate, and scarf down some damn good Canadian food. But as soon as Sergei voiced the idea, she realized that all those things were embodied in a hug.

"What changes would you think of making to the place?" Rhonda asked. She was paranoid after listening to the other buyers Cheryl had brought around. Ideas from white linen tablecloths and candles, to psychedelic murals, to nouveau cuisine, to self-serve buffet. Worst: removing the counter and stools, replacing the black and white tiles with slate. Curtains on the windows. Changing the red Naugahyde booth seating to tartan fabric.

Sure, she wanted to sell the café, but she didn't want it destroyed. She shuddered at visions of being tarred and feathered by the regular diners.

Sergei gazed at the interior, taking in the red and silver counter stools, the tiled floor, the booths along one wall, the Tiffany lamps above each booth. "Nothing. I don't think I'd change a thing. It just screams 'welcome,' doesn't it?"

He strolled to the kitchen. "I might switch out an appliance or two, but only after I see how what you've got here works." He picked up a menu and studied it. "Yep, looks about right to me. Might add a couple specials, like pierogies, or nalesniki, for the Europeans among us."

Rhonda's mouth watered when he mentioned pierogies. "Could you make me some pierogies today? I can try them out on the diners. See what the regulars think?"

He removed his jacket. "Got an apron? And show me where the flour is. And potatoes."

———

THE DINNER SPECIAL OF PIEROGIES, fried onions, bacon, and sour cream was a roaring hit. Rhonda introduced Sergei to her diners as "Tiffany's Guest Chef and Pierogi King." He received a standing ovation.

After the dinner rush, Rhonda and Sergei sat at a small table near the back of the café. "I'd say the regulars like your cooking," Rhonda said.

"It felt good to cook for them."

Rhonda said, "Why do you want to move here? I ask because that fellow in the booth over there is Gabe Gabrieli, one of the owners of The Peak Bar across the street. He's from Eau Claire in Alberta. He misses the big blue skies, says the mountains make him feel trapped. Are you sure you can handle it?"

The constant smile left Sergei's face. "Ahh, I lost my wife last year. She and I ran our diner side by side for forty years. I can't look at it without missing her. I wasn't handling the loss too well. In fact, some said I wasn't handling it at all. The kids did what they called an intervention and convinced me to take a break, try some place different. So here I am."

"Would you be looking at the café as a long-term investment?"

"Certainly for at least a year. And if things don't work out, then I'd think about selling the business."

Rhonda's face must have shown her concern about another sale of the café within a year, because Sergei raised his hands and said, "I can see this business means a lot to you. If I decided to sell, I could give you the first option to buy it back, and failing that, I'd let you veto any buyer who didn't measure up. What do you say?"

40

Saturday, July 24, 2010

TIFFANY'S CAFÉ

FOR A SATURDAY, things were slow at the café. Rhonda was happy about that. Like an idiot, she had said okay when the kids mentioned they wanted to go hiking with Owen. She even fixed them a picnic lunch. She'd been a total bag before Frank got home and knew that David and Roxy had suffered along with her. In fact, Rhonda had taken her worries out on them. Scolded them for being late for a shift. Picked at the jobs they were doing bussing tables and managing diners.

They were wonderful kids, and Rhonda loved them with all her heart. So why did she take things out on them? Just because she was having a time of it, didn't mean she had to make their lives a misery.

She said, "Great idea!" when they mentioned a hike. And then she made their favorite sandwiches, added muffins and apples, and sent them off with a grin on her face.

All the time hoping she and Frank could manage the café alone. Luckily, most diners knew the menu by heart, knew to get their own coffees at the rack of thermoses, knew to buss their own tables when David and Roxy weren't at the café. All Rhonda had to do was cook and deliver their meals. Frank had been "volunteered" to take orders and man the cash register.

Maybe selling to Sergei was the thing to do. Several diners had mentioned last night's pierogies, saying they hoped it would be a regular on the menu.

"Let me think about it for a day or two," Rhonda had said when Sergei suggested she could buy the café back from him after a year. Maybe. If things didn't work out for him.

He was the perfect buyer, so why wasn't she jumping at the offer? Rhonda looked at Gabe, sitting beneath one of her Tiffany lampshades in his favorite booth at the back of the café. She knew she should get Frank to fix that banshee toilet, but then Gabe would be cheated out of the enjoyment he got by slapping the "out of order" sign on the stall door. She and Gabe had special conversations in that booth.

She grabbed a water jug and moved along the counter to the far end where Anders Thorvaldsen sat. She topped up his water glass. He looked up from his magazine. "Thanks kiddo," he said. Kiddo. Perhaps to Anders, everyone was a kiddo. But she loved that he called her that. How often would she get to hear that endearment from him in the future?

She snapped out of her reverie when the door banged open and Sergei Kravachenko strolled in. He beckoned to Rhonda.

When she joined him at the counter by the espresso machine, he said, "So I'm getting bored hanging around town. I mean, I've seen almost all the sights. I know every business on Main Street by heart and who owns them. I've memorized all the real estate listings on the window across the way."

Rhonda folded her arms and nodded. Here it comes. He was about to tell her the town was too small for him. That High River looks like a big city compared to this backwater village. "Yeah, the town's compact, shall we say?"

"In a good way, though," Sergei said. "What I mean is, I see you're pretty much alone today. I was thinking. Can I do some cooking?"

She tossed an apron at him. "Minimum wage is all I can pay. Even for top-notch chefs."

He rolled his shirt sleeves above his elbows and flexed his fingers like a pianist preparing for a performance. The Ukrainian trident tattooed on his forearm rippled. "Geez, Rhonda," Sergei said, "I'm so bored, I'll do it for nothing."

"Done. One word of advice. The burger sauce? Ingredients are in a notebook on the top shelf in the walk-in fridge. Secret. So don't let the rabble worm it out of you."

As soon as Sergei took over the grill, Rhonda headed to the front of the café and opened a drawer in the cabinet beside the cash register. Her kitchen sink drawer. The place she stashed pens, elastic bands, sticky notes, a flashlight, random batteries, keys that no longer opened any lock in the café, but she couldn't throw out just in case. Time to sort out the mess. Get a head start on packing up her business. Her stomach sank at the thought.

Tucked beneath the flashlight was a piece of looseleaf paper. Folded in four. She couldn't remember putting it into the drawer, but then her memory had been iffy lately. All the stress she was under. Maybe David or Roxy stashed it there.

She unfolded the paper and read the handwritten note.

"I said you were next. Saturday, the day Karma comes knocking."

Rhonda felt a cold sweat break out. What the hell was this?

Rhonda turned and waved at her husband, who was lugging a bin of dirty dishes into the kitchen. "Frank! Frank, look at this."

Gabe raised his head from his paperback at the sound of Rhonda's voice. Anders Thorvaldsen put his knife and fork down and stared at her.

Frank hurried over, and she thrust the note into his hands. When he read it, his face paled. "Jesus, Rho."

41

Saturday, July 24, 2010

TIFFANY'S CAFÉ

When Gabe heard Rhonda's voice hit the higher octave that he knew meant she was either completely pissed off or frantic, he put his book aside and studied her face. Panic.

Then he watched Frank read whatever was on the paper Rhonda had given him, saw Frank go pale, and watched his hands shake.

Gabe slid from the booth and hurried over to the couple.

"Hey, is everything okay?" he said.

Rhonda grabbed the paper from Frank and shoved it at Gabe. "Look at this! It's talking about today."

Gabe read the note, picked up on the mention of karma, and quickly compared the handwriting to the picture he'd taken of the dry erase board in Wilfred Stillwater's hospital room. It looked the same. "Make sure you aren't alone today, Rhonda. Stick close to Frank."

"What?" she said.

"Stan found a note with karma on it in his parents' belongings. Someone scrawled karma on the whiteboard in Wilfred Stillwater's hospital room. And printed the word on the sailboat that Lara Quinn had rented."

"Omigod, is there a crazy maniac in town? You knew about this, and you didn't tell me?"

Gabe raised his hands. "I didn't want to cause a panic and had no reason to think you'd be in danger."

"Oh shit," Rhonda said. "I got a text about karma a while ago."

"You didn't tell me that."

"I thought it was Russian bots. A scam."

Gabe said, "Let's think about this. Why would someone target you, Rhonda? What's the connection with the other people who have been attacked?" He pulled his notebook out and flipped through the pages. Then he read the names: "Wilfred Stillwater. Lara Quinn. Leonard and Verna Wurtz. And then a guy named Driesden—according to a letter Maxine got over at the paper, he would have been one of the victims, but he died before the killer could get to him."

"No connection I know," Rhonda said. "I know the Wurtzes. Lara Quinn was in the café a time or two. I definitely don't know Wilfred Stillwater. Or Driesden, although his name is familiar."

"Driesden was a lawyer," Gabe said.

"Oh right," Rhonda said. "Ages ago, I was on a jury, and I think he was one of the lawyers in the trial. I could be wrong."

Then Rhonda gasped. "I don't know Wilfred Stillwater, but I know Theo. And Theo was on that jury with me."

She slapped her hands up to her face. "Oh, oh, oh, and Kathaleen Quinn was the judge. I remember it was her first big criminal trial."

Frank said, "I recall that time. Had to do all the cooking for the kids and me because Rhonda was sequestered. Wasn't Stan Wurtz the key prosecution witness?"

"Oh shit," Rhonda said. "Is someone targeting people from that trial? But that can't be right. It was more than ten years ago, maybe fifteen. Why would they wait that long?"

"Who was the accused?" Gabe said.

Rhonda's face went blank. She stared at Gabe, looked at Frank, and then back at Gabe. "I can't remember. My memory has gone all to hell lately." She tapped on her head with a fist. "C'mon, c'mon. Think Rhonda!"

When Rhonda began pacing, pounding on her head, and talking to herself, Gabe used his cell phone to phone Kathaleen Quinn.

"Hey, judge," he said when she answered his call. "Do you remember your first criminal trial? One with a jury?"

"No one forgets their first trial," Quinn said. "It was embezzlement."

"Do you remember the name of the accused?"

"Of course. Al Campbell. I sentenced him to seven years."

"He'd be out now for sure?"

Quinn sighed into the phone. "He died in prison. Legionnaire's Disease, I think. Tragic, because he was about to be released on parole."

"Okay, thanks," Gabe said. He was about to end the call when he said, "One more thing. Did he have family?"

"A wife. I believe her name was Louise. She was in court every day. Threw a tantrum when he was convicted. Swore Al had been set up, and that everyone had ganged up on him. We had to have the bailiffs remove her from the courtroom."

"Guess you don't know where she is now, eh?"

"No, sorry. Does this have anything to do with Lara's death?"

"It could. I'm still trying to figure it out."

"Let me know if I can help further," Quinn said. "And good luck."

Gabe ended the call, and then quickly phoned Sergeant LeBlanc. For once, LeBlanc answered the call instead of letting it go to voicemail, as he tended to do whenever Gabe pestered him. "Gabrieli! What kind of trouble are you in today?"

"The serious kind, LeBlanc. Can you check out a woman for me? I think she's here in Cheakamus killing people."

LeBlanc sucked in his breath. "*Merde*. Give me the details. I'll get on it. Stand by."

Gabe ended the call with LeBlanc and filled Rhonda and Frank in on the conversations.

"If this Louise went off the rails at the trial," Rhonda said, "maybe she's seeking revenge. But why now, so long after the trial?"

Gabe said, "Beats me. It's weird." He was silent for a beat and then said, "And the other thing that's weird is that she's not going directly after the people involved in the trial."

"What do you mean?" Rhonda asked. She grabbed the paper from Frank's hand. "It says right here. 'I said you'd be next.' She's coming after me."

Gabe shook his head. "I don't think so. Look at the victims: Stan Wurtz's parents. Theo Stillwater's father. Judge Quinn's sister."

Rhonda paled and staggered. Frank grabbed her arm. "That means," Rhonda said. "That means she could be after Frank? Or, omigod, or David or Roxy!"

Rhonda spun in circles, clasping her hands to her face. "Frank, our kids! They are out there on a hike and there's a maniac somewhere."

"Calm down, Rho," Frank said. "We'll find them. Where did they go?"

"I don't know! They didn't say. Just that they were going hiking with Owen."

Gabe said, "I think I know where to find them."

42

Saturday, July 24, 2010
PRIM'S FOLLY

THE THREE OF them had piled into Owen's van for the drive from Cheakamus to Granite Mountain. He'd told David and Roxy that it would save the environment if they went together. Of course, he'd be making the return trip alone, but the other two didn't need to know that.

He parked in the public lot at the base of Granite Mountain, near the logging road that snaked up the mountain to the mine, about halfway to the summit. The Folly, people called it. The story was that Silas Jones had been looking for gold and staked the claim because his wife, Primrose, loved the view from the site. When the site proved to hold only tungsten, worthless at the time, and no gold, Silas named the mining claim "Prim's Folly." He kept the claim, and maintained it, however, because Primrose loved it.

Now it was abandoned. Old man Jones was long dead, and his widow was somewhere on the west coast. In a rinky-dink town, probably just like Cheakamus. Small. Boring. A good place to be away from.

He didn't voice his opinion to David and Roxy. They didn't need to know that either.

They hiked along the logging road, chattering about

summer plans, the upcoming school year, Roxy's gymnastics competition next Tuesday, and more. The picnic lunch, which consisted of sandwiches, muffins, apples, occupied a small cooler bag that David and Owen carried between them.

"Jack's going to meet us here later," Roxy said.

That stopped Owen in his tracks. "What?"

"Jack's coming. I invited him."

Owen debated postponing his plans. But then he remembered Stillwater could wake up from his coma any minute. And, Jack was on Owen's list. If he worked quickly, he could take care of Roxy and David now. And then just hang out, waiting for Jack to show up.

He nodded. Yep, that would work.

When they reached the Folly, Roxy pulled a small blanket from her pack and spread it on the ground. The guys dropped the cooler bag on the blanket.

"What should we do?" Roxy said. "Explore the forest? Look for gold?"

"There's no gold here. The Viking knows every gold site in the mountains, and he doesn't even come by this area anymore," David said.

"Let's check out the old headframe," Owen said.

Roxy snorted. "It's boarded up, or hadn't you noticed?"

"No, someone smashed the lock," Owen said. "I was poking around, and the door is open. We can get inside, maybe look down the shaft into the mine. What d'ya say?"

Roxy shivered and hugged herself. "Old mines smell bad. Ever smelled the tunnels at the Evergold Mine on Rimrock? Yuk."

"C'mon. We're not gonna go into tunnels, we're just gonna take a peek down the hole. Try to guess how deep it is. You can hold your breath for ten or fifteen seconds, so you won't smell anything."

David nudged Roxy. "Yeah, c'mon Rox. It'll be cool."

She shook her head. "You guys go ahead. I'll just relax here in the sun."

"Are you afraid?" Owen asked.

"Afraid? Of what? Some dumb old hole in the ground?"

"A deep hole. Maybe one we can't get out of if we slip and fall. That's it, isn't it? I guess all those stories about fearless Roxanne Zalesko are hogwash."

"I'm not chicken!" Roxy said. "I just don't see the point of staring at a dark hole."

Owen threw up his hands and blew out a breath. "Because maybe there is gold at the bottom of the shaft. What if there's a way we could go down there and see for ourselves? Don't you think we should at least look?"

"David just told you there's no gold here."

Owen said, "That's right, I forgot. But maybe there are antique tools down there. Maybe we could bring them up and sell them. Or give them to Mrs. Rocque's museum."

"C'mon Rox," David said again. "Let's look."

Roxanne sighed and stood up, brushing her jeans off as she did so. "Alright. Alright. Geez, what is it with guys and holes in the ground?"

The three began the long trudge uphill to the decrepit headframe.

"I used to live hereabouts," Owen said.

"Really? Where?" asked Roxy.

"In Cheakamus. Until I was five or six. My mom, my dad, and me."

"Then your family moved away?"

Owen kicked at a stone like it was a soccer ball and watched it skitter down the hill. "My mom and me. We moved to Ontario."

"Did something happen to your dad?" Roxy said.

"You could say that." They were about two minutes away from the headframe, he figured, if they kept up this pace. "Anyway, things were shitty after we moved. And they got worse after my father died. Mom had a tough time finding jobs and she hit the bottle. I tried hard to help, but I was a kid. You can't buy many groceries with money from mowing lawns and shoveling snow."

"Man, that sounds tough. But you look like you came out of it okay?"

Owen grimaced. "Mom died when I was eleven. Drove our car into a ravine. I was in it but survived. Anyhoooooo, long story short, I survived seven years of foster care and when I aged out, they gave me a few hundred bucks that I used to buy a bus ticket to come back here."

They reached the top of the hill and the level ground where the headframe sat. The door creaked loudly when Owen pulled it open. Sunlight spilled into the area beyond the door through spaces between the boards surrounding the base, creating an eerie scene of strips of dark and light. Owen leaned through the doorway and checked out the open area. David and Roxy peered around him.

"Nothing much here," David said.

"Smells bad," Roxy said. "I told you so."

Owen entered the space. "Look! That must be the shaft, eh? They've covered it with a lid. Let's lift it!"

David and Roxy joined him inside. David studied the lid. "Looks like whoever bust the lock on the door broke the locks on the lid, too. Maybe modern-day pirates are storing their treasures down the shaft!"

"Or drugs," Roxy said. She looked over her shoulder at the doorway. "This could be dangerous if there are drug dealers around. We should go."

Owen laughed. "I don't think there are drugs down there. It would be too much work to get to them when the dealer needs to restock. I mean, they'd have to climb the hill, open the lid, get down the shaft and then back up."

He shook his head. "Nope. And even if there are drugs, the dealers wouldn't do all that work. They'd get some dumb kid to do it for them. And the three of us could manage a scared little kid for sure."

Roxy exhaled loudly. "Yeah, I guess I'm seeing ghosts. So, are we gonna lift the lid or what?"

Owen moved around the metal lid to stand on the far side of the open space. "Roxy, come help me lift and David can lift the other side."

Roxy joined Owen and bent down to grip the underside of the lid. She tugged at it and felt it give slightly. "Doesn't feel too heavy."

Owen said, "On three?"

The three of them gripped the lid, and Owen counted. On three, they lifted the lid. "Hurray!" Owen said. "That was easy. Let's put the lid beside the shaft."

After they set the lid aside, Owen peered down the shaft. "Dark and deep. But at least there's a ladder for anyone who gets stuck down there."

He backed away from the shaft. "So you asked if something happened to my father?"

Roxy turned to face him, her back to the shaft. David stood where he was, on the opposite side of the shaft, close to the doorway. "What happened?" Roxy said.

Owen smiled grimly. "He died. But before that, some people said he embezzled money from his job. Then a cop arrested him, and at the trial he was convicted and sent to prison. He didn't do it, but they convicted him anyway."

"That's awful," Roxy said. "Is that why you moved away?"

Owen nodded. "So just before Dad was going to be let out of prison on parole, he got a virus. Legionnaire's Disease. And he died. And then everything that was already shitty got even shittier."

"I'm sorry," Roxy said.

"Yeah man, that's rough," said David.

"Mom kept telling me karma would make things even.

That all the people who banded together to set my father up for something he didn't do would be paid back by karma."

"You believe in karma?" asked Roxy.

"I waited and waited for karma to make things right. But finally, I knew karma needed help. I'm karma's helper. I'm making things right."

"What do you mean, you're karma's helper?" Roxy said.

Owen began pacing by the exterior wall of the area surrounding the shaft. "I'm The Helper. Everyone who ganged up against my father. Everyone who played a part in making my mom and me suffer. They're finding out what it's like to lose someone they love. They're learning to suffer like Mom and I did."

"What? You're hurting people?"

Owen approached Roxy. He yelled in her face. "Killing them. I'm killing them. And you're next because your mother was on the jury. Rhonda. Nice, friendly Rhonda, who everyone in town thinks is a saint, voted to send my dad to prison!"

Roxy sucked in a breath and turned away. She took one step before Owen shoved her. With a yelp, she toppled heels over head into the shaft.

"Roxy! No!" David shouted.

43

Saturday, July 24, 2010
TIFFANY'S CAFÉ

GABE SCROLLED through his text messages and showed Rhonda the one from Jack. "Prim's Folly. Jack canceled lunch with me so he could meet up with Roxy at Prim's Folly. Do you know where that is?"

"Somewhere on Granite Mountain," Frank said.

"I know the Folly." The Viking, Anders Thorvaldsen, rose from his stool at the far end of the counter and joined them. "I heard you talking. I can tell you about the Folly. Easy enough to get to, especially if you go up the logging road. About halfway up Granite. An old tungsten mine."

Gabe asked, "Any cliff faces to fall from?"

"Nope. Just rolling grassy hilltops. However…"

"There are tunnels, right? Am I gonna have to go crawling through mine tunnels, Anders?" Even thinking about tunnels made Gabe's skin prickle and his vision narrow.

The Viking shook his head. "Well, mebbe. But they closed that mine way back in the sixties. And as far as I remember, the entrance is a shaft under a headframe."

Gabe knew about headframes. Greta Rocque had given him a lesson about the structure last fall.

He hated underground anything unless it was an enormous parkade. Those he tried to avoid, but didn't outright hate them. But mines? Tunnels? Mine shafts descending into the dark? Made him want to just fall down in a faint.

"I heard the last owner of the Folly had sealed the shaft," The Viking said. "That was Greta's father's cheating partner. Stole the Folly from Silas, Greta's dad. Unscrupulous, he was."

Gabe was breathing easier now that he knew the shaft was sealed. The hunt for the young hikers would be above ground then. Something Gabe could easily handle.

"No way for someone to go down the shaft? Or fall into it?" Gabe said.

The Viking shrugged. "Never say never, sonny. If the guy shut down the mine the way the government wanted back then, he should have put a concrete plug over the shaft. Then you'd be sure no one could get into trouble. But that guy?" The Viking shook his head and grimaced. "That guy didn't play by the rules. I checked out the Folly's headframe a few years ago. There's hoarding around the base, like there should be. There's a door built into the hoarding, but it was locked when I checked it. I hoisted myself above the hoarding and peeked inside. There's a lid over the shaft, but it's a metal one."

Gabe opened his mouth to comment but was interrupted by his phone. The display said "LeBlanc."

Gabe answered the call. "Gabrieli here."

LeBlanc said, "I checked out that case. Guy's wife was Louise. She's dead, drove off the side of a mountain. Had a kid in the car but he survived. He'd be nineteen or twenty now. Owen Campbell. He's all that's left of the Judge's first trial."

Gabe asked LeBlanc to get Lightheart over to Prim's Folly. "Maybe a couple of ambulances, too, eh?"

LeBlanc signed off and Gabe turned to the group. "It's not Campbell's wife who's been doing this. It's his kid. Owen."

"Owen? Owen, who went hiking with my kids today?" Rhonda said, her voice shaking. "Owen, who I hired because I thought he was too skinny and needed all the free food he could get here? Omigod! We have to go find them. Now!"

44

Saturday, July 24, 2010
PRIM'S FOLLY

OWEN RACED AROUND THE SHAFT, hoping to tackle David before he got away.

But after Roxy fell into the shaft, David had turned and split. Out the door and downhill. When Owen charged through the doorway, he saw David was a third of the way to the blanket they'd put down. He should have remembered that David was a star on the high school track team.

He gave chase, desperate to catch him.

Then, a stroke of luck. David tripped and fell. He got to his feet but then fell again, crying out and grabbing at his ankle. Far out! Good old track star David had probably stepped in a gopher hole. Maybe broke his ankle. Even if he'd merely twisted it, that was good for Owen.

David got to his feet once more. He took off downhill. Hopping more than running. So, no broken ankle. But definitely painful enough to slow David down.

Owen switched his pace into full steam ahead. Less than a minute later, he tackled David. They whumped onto the ground. David leaped up, ready for a fight.

Owen shot a right fist at David's head. David jerked away, lost his balance, and fell backward.

Owen threw himself on top of David and punched him in the head. But David bucked his legs and torso, heaving Owen to the side.

They scrambled up. Owen launched a stream of rights and lefts into David's body and then pasted him with a vicious uppercut. David fell backward onto the ground. Out cold.

Owen leaned over, braced his hands on his knees, and gulped in air. He was out of shape. Thank karma his other victims hadn't fought back. Of course, they had all been older. Except Lara Quinn. She was middle-aged and strong enough that Owen had to be careful when he swung that bat. Pretended he was Babe Ruth and hit for the fences.

Now he had David to deal with. Simple enough. Haul him back up the hill to the headframe and dump him down the shaft so he could spend eternity with his sister. Done deal.

He got his second wind and straightened.

Wham! Something landed on his back and damn near knocked the wind out of him. His first thought was a bear. Omigod, he couldn't be bear food, not now. Not when he was so close to making things right.

A voice pierced his thoughts. A high-pitched angry voice. "You bastard! What did you do to David?"

Not a bear then. A person was on his back, pounding on his head.

Roxy? Sounded like her. But she was down the shaft. He knew she was. He'd pushed her into it. How...? He turned in a circle, fast, trying to dislodge her from his back.

She wrapped her legs tighter around his waist and clung on, shouting. "You thought you killed me? No way, asshole. I'm not a gymnast for nothing. I grabbed a rung on the ladder and hung on. Then climbed out. Easy peasy."

She yelled at her brother. "David! David! I'm here. Hang on. Wake up. Please don't die."

Owen grabbed Roxy's shins and pried them away from his body. Then he spun quickly and threw himself forward, head over heels, onto the ground. Roxy ended up on her back beneath him, gasping for breath.

"Hey!" a male voice said. "What's going on?"

45

Saturday, July 24, 2010
PRIM'S FOLLY

GABE WAS the first to arrive at the parking lot at the base of Granite Mountain. The Viking had told him the Folly could be accessed from the logging road that forked off to the left from the parking lot.

He put the truck into four-wheel drive, patted the dash, and said, "Right, Three. It's your special day. You get to go off road, up a mountain, and into the bush. I'm coming along so don't do anything stupid like get stuck. I don't want to have to dig you out, hear?"

He gunned the motor and turned onto the logging road, bouncing over the ruts and gullies that had not seen maintenance for years. The sun was blocked by towering evergreens. Branches reached out and scraped the sides of the truck. A familiar tingle started on Gabe's skin. "Deep breaths," he said out loud. "There's daylight just ahead. Nothing to get all uptight about."

Gabe breathed in slowly, counting to four. Then held his breath and counted to four. Exhaled to the count of four. Over and over, he concentrated on breathing in and out to a four-count. Eventually, his heart rate slowed, and the tingling eased. Daylight appeared at the end of the trail. Gabe wasn't sure whether the breathing exercise had calmed him, or the sight of an exit from this tunnel of trees.

He exited the trail onto a grassy hillside. At the top of the hill sat an ancient headframe. Almost a replica of the mockup that last year had graced the entry to the Evergold Mining Museum on Rimrock. Greta's museum. But this one was the real thing and much larger.

Movement on the hillside, about halfway to the crest, caught Gabe's attention. A huddle of people. He picked out Jack in the melee. And a girl with long dark hair. Had to be Roxy. Both were doing a dance with another fellow? David?

No. That was Owen.

Where was David?

Gabe shifted gears and pressed down on the accelerator. Three spun his back wheels for a moment, then the tires grabbed, and the truck climbed the hill. As he drove, Gabe scanned the hill for signs of David. Then he spotted a figure. Prone, but struggling to rise.

Gabe slammed on his brakes, turned off the ignition, and leaped from the truck.

"David? You okay?"

"Yeah. Go help Roxy!"

Gabe turned toward the threesome about a hundred yards away. Jack, Roxy and Owen. Scuffling, shoving, and yelling. He rushed forward, limping from his wonky knee, but gaining ground quickly.

When Owen spotted Gabe, he turned and sprinted for the headframe. Jack, Roxy, and Gabe gave chase.

When they reached the top of the hill, Owen had disappeared. The door to the headframe enclosure was closed.

Gabe stood outside the door. "Owen! Come out here and we can help you sort all this out."

"No, you can't! No one can."

Gabe wrenched the door open, leaping backward to avoid

the flying objects he expected Owen to pitch through the doorway. Nothing happened.

Gabe peered around the door into the dim interior. Less than ten feet square, with bare wood walls and an open space that surrounded the mine shaft. Owen stood at the far side of the shaft, staring into its dark depths.

Gabe's stomach flipped. The toes of Owen's sneakers were over the edge of the shaft. The distance from the doorway to where Owen stood was more than six feet. No way could Gabe grab Owen if he lost his balance.

Gabe forced himself to speak calmly. "Hey, Owen. It's just me."

When Owen raised his eyes, Gabe read the loss and pain they held. He took two steps through the doorway.

Owen shouted. "Stop! Or I'll jump."

"Okay, no prob. Can we talk?"

"There's nothing to talk about. I've been helping karma get back at people who ruined my life. And my mom's life. And now I guess my job's done." He shrugged. "Well, mostly."

"Who ruined things for you and your mom? Wasn't it your dad, Owen?"

"Nononono! Dad didn't do anything. Mom told me people set him up and then everyone else around here ganged up and sent him to jail. Where he died! And then everything got terrible."

"But you got through it, hey? I mean, here you are, healthy and with a job and friends. Isn't that worth sticking around for?"

"That will all be gone after people find out what I've done. They'll gang up on me just like they did to my dad."

While Owen ranted, Gabe shuffled a foot closer to the shaft. Maybe he could leap across the divide and tackle Owen. He tried not to think of how far he would fall if he miscalculated the leap.

Roxy was the gymnast. David was the track star. They could make that leap without blinking. Gabe had a sore knee and hadn't tried the long jump since high school. Twenty years ago. And the long jump required a running start.

Two feet of ground between Gabe and the near edge of the shaft. Four feet or more of an open gap to reach Owen on the far edge. So max two steps, from a standing start, and then a lunge.

Jack and the others stood just outside the doorway. He hoped they were paying attention and would help him grab Owen. Or lower a very long rope to him if he missed.

"Just leave me here," Owen said, his voice full of regret. "So I can make peace with—"

"If you're thinking of making peace with the Head Honcho, then step away from the shaft. I've had a few conversations with the Big Guy and lemme tell you he's much easier to get along with when you're not trying to jump into the abyss. He's all about responsibility, Owen. As in, you gotta own up to your failings and start trying to make up for them. When the Head Honcho sees that you're honestly trying to square your mistakes, He's been known to lend a hand."

"What are you, a priest? Get outta here. Leave me alone."

"The last thing I am is a priest. Not even priestly. I just know about mistakes and how they can ruin your life if you let them. Let me to be the hand that the Big Guy wants to lend you. What do you say?"

Gabe held out his right hand.

Owen bowed his head and sighed. He looked up through the tower to the bright blue sky above. Then he shrugged and stepped backward away from the edge, onto the solid ground beside the shaft.

Gabe let out the breath he'd been holding. He kept his hand out toward Owen and said, "Good. Good. Come around here and I'll walk you outside. We can sit in the grass and talk, okay?"

Owen smiled and walked slowly around the shaft toward him.

Gabe watched Owen approach. Another step and Owen would be within grabbing distance.

Owen stopped and said, "It's been nice chatting. See you on the other side?" Then he dove headfirst into the shaft.

When Gabe heard the words "other side," he lunged. Not to leap across the divide, but to reach into it and grab whatever parts of Owen he could. He felt Owen's shirt brush his fingertips. Gabe clutched the bottom of the shirt. He felt it come loose from inside Owen's cargo shorts. But he held on.

He heard popping. Two pops. The shirt felt looser. Gabe realized buttons had popped.

Owen fell another foot, his weight pulling Gabe partly over the edge of the shaft. Gabe yelled. "Jack, David, help!"

Instantly, he felt their hands on him, grabbing his belt and boots and pulling back to anchor him.

Gabe's grip on Owen's shirt held for the moment. Owen's fall had stopped, and Gabe heard the thump as the kid banged into the ladder on the side of the shaft.

"Okay," Gabe said. "I've got you. So how about you use the ladder to climb back up here?"

Owen hung there, dangling from Gabe's handful of shirt.

Gabe heard another button pop.

Gabe's hand cramped, and he longed to flex his fingers. Owen struggled and then went limp. "Okay, alright. Let me get my hands on the ladder."

Gabe breathed in slowly, wondering how many buttons were left on the shirt. He held tight as Owen swung his body around and grabbed a rung. "Okay, you can let go," Owen said.

"No chance," Gabe said. "I'm hanging on until I see you out here on solid ground."

Owen gasped. "Give me a minute, man. I gotta catch my

breath. I've got my feet on the ladder now, so I'm just gonna stand here a bit and breathe."

It was so dark in the shaft that all Gabe could see of Owen was the top of his head, and the white fabric of his shirt, which had ridden up when Gabe grabbed it. He could hear Owen breathing heavily.

"How're you doing?" Gabe asked.

"Good. Another few seconds and I should be good to go."

Gabe felt, rather than saw, Owen moving quietly below him. Doing something with his hands. Maybe he was trying to get a better grip on the ladder.

Then Owen raised his face toward Gabe. "I really can't stay, Gabe. They'll lock me up forever. I'd rather die."

He raised his arms and stepped backward off the ladder. One of Owen's arms slipped out of his now fully unbuttoned shirt. "Owen, no!"

Gabe clenched his hand tighter on Owen's shirt, but heard a tearing sound as the fabric gave way under Owen's weight. Then there was nothing. And then a whump.

"Noooo!" Gabe lay there, holding the remnants of Owen's shirt.

46

Saturday, July 24, 2010
PRIM'S FOLLY

GABE STARED down the shaft into the darkness below. How deep was the hole?

"Jack! Run to my truck and get my flashlight and first aid kit. And there should be a rope in the truck bed."

Roxy put her hand on Gabe's shoulder. "I'm going down there," she said. Gabe moved away from the opening and Roxy scrambled over the edge onto the ladder. Thirty seconds later she shouted.

"Owen's hurt bad! I counted forty-five rungs on my way down. I'm guessing it's about twenty feet deep here."

"Right." Gabe said. He swung his legs over the gap and placed his feet on one of the ladder's rungs. When the wood creaked under his weight, sweat popped out on his brow. If the ladder gave way, he'd fall. Maybe kill Roxanne and Owen if he landed on them. Maybe break a few hundred of his own bones as well.

Plus, it was dark down there and confined. Sure, only kids were afraid of the dark. But this darkness was narrow and enclosed. Like a coffin. His vision blurred at the edges and a familiar tingling began in his hands.

Gabe sucked in a deep breath. Held it. And then exhaled

to the count of four. "Look," the rational side of his brain said, "You did it at the Evergold Mine. You went under a mountain of rock. You can do it again, and this time it's not even tunnels. It's merely a twenty-foot hole. Piece of cake."

The terrified, claustrophobic side of his brain said, "The first responders are on their way. LeBlanc has mobilized everyone. You can hold the fort here, at the top of the shaft."

"Gabe?" Roxy called. "Are you coming down?"

He breathed slowly and closed his eyes. And when he opened them, Jack stood in the entrance of the shed. "Here's the stuff," Jack said and handed the flashlight to Gabe. "Are you going down?"

Gabe illuminated the light. His vision cleared and the tingling eased. He pointed the beam down the shaft and spotted Roxanne looking up at him. He stuck the stem of the flashlight into the back pocket of his jeans, so its light shined upward. Then he gritted his teeth, nodded to Jack, and said, "Yeah. Can you lower the first aid kit to Roxanne?"

As he descended the creaking ladder, Gabe refused to look down. He focused his eyes on Jack standing at the top of the opening, and the reassuring light cast by the flashlight. He counted the rungs and when he reached thirty-five, he stopped, grabbed the flashlight from his pocket, and pointed it toward Roxanne. His breathing relaxed and his grip on the ladder loosened when he realized he stood a mere four feet from the ground, and the space in which Roxanne stood was an enormous cavern cut from the surrounding rock. When his light picked out tunnel openings leading away from the cavern, Gabe guessed this cavern had been a staging area for the mine operations.

Owen lay in a twisted heap about three feet away from the base of the ladder. By the time Gabe descended the remaining four feet, Roxanne had grabbed the first aid kit that Jack had lowered, opened it, and extracted several bandages. She pressed them to the back of Owen's head to staunch the flow of blood. She glanced at Gabe as he knelt beside Owen, and shook her head, mouthing, "It's bad."

Gabe placed the flashlight on the ground nearby, where its beam dimly illuminated the immediate area. When he touched Owen's shoulder, Owen reached his right hand out. "Hey, Mr. Gabrieli. I guess I screwed up. I'm still alive."

"Hang on, Owen," Gabe said, clasping his hand. "Help's on the way."

Owen sighed. "Help maybe. But not hope. I gave that up when I was eleven."

"Why?"

"You know Mom tried to kill us? Me and her. When I was eleven. She said we'd be better off dead. But she died and I survived. And then I was alone, and they put me into a foster home. I hoped things would be better, that I would be happy with my new family."

Owen winced. "Ohh, everything hurts. I'm so tired." His eyelids fluttered.

"Hang on, Owen," Gabe said. "What happened with your new family?"

Owen coughed. Blood trickled from his mouth. "Nothing. They left me alone. The only thing they loved about me was the check they got every month. Mom was a lush but at least she loved me. I wish…"

"What?"

"I wish karma had done what Mom said it would. Teach those people how awful it was to lose someone they loved, just like what happened to her and me when Dad went away. She told me what they'd done to Dad. Framing him, lying in court, ganging up with the lawyers, and the jury, and the judge to send him away. I waited and waited for karma to do its job."

Jack shouted down the shaft. "Gabe! Help is here."

Owen tightened his grip on Gabe's hand and smiled at him. "You know what? I think Mom was right. It would have been better to be dead all those years." He closed his eyes. "Much better."

His grip loosened.

"Owen, stay here," Gabe said.

Two paramedics bounded down the ladder. While one unpacked equipment, the other pushed Gabe and Roxanne to the side, and examined Owen. She felt for a pulse and then put a stethoscope to Owen's chest and listened for a minute.

When she finally raised her head, her face was somber. "I'm sorry," she said. "He's gone."

47

Saturday, July 24, 2010
CHEAKAMUS, BC

RHONDA AND FRANK bundled their kids into their car and headed toward Cheakamus. The ambulance carrying Owen's body had left the site an hour earlier, while the police took statements from the three teenagers and Gabe.

Thank heaven the kids were okay. They were shaken by the experience and upset that Owen had died. But, aside from David's shiner and bruises, they were physically fine.

After Rhonda had hugged her kids when she arrived at Prim's Folly, she had spotted Gabe standing alone beside the old headframe, staring off to the mountains in the west. She strode over to him, calling out to him on her way.

Gabe swiped at his eyes before he turned to face her. She hugged him and said, "Thanks for looking out for my babies."

He held the hug for a moment and then backed away. When he smiled at her his eyes were wet, the unshed tears turning them a deeper, darker blue. "Hey, they had things well in hand by the time I got here. I heard Roxanne leaped onto Owen's back to protect David. Kind of a cool sister to have."

Rhonda grinned. "Yep. She's a keeper." Then her smiled died and she said, "Even though Owen was a killer, I'm sorry we lost him."

Gabe had nodded. "From what he told me, Owen was lost years ago."

Now, Rhonda's thoughts turned back to her family and their future.

She realized she'd left Sergei Kravachenko in the café without a word other than, "Can you manage for a bit?" She wasn't concerned. Instinctively, she knew the man could handle anything the diners threw at him.

He was the perfect buyer, but Rhonda didn't want to let go of the café. Deep down, she knew that was the reason she had found fault with all the other buyers. She didn't want any of them touching her baby.

She turned in her seat and faced David and Roxy, who were in the back. "Listen, kids, I have something to tell you."

They quickly raised their eyes to hers. She saw fear in their expressions. "Don't worry, it's nothing disastrous. Merely life changing. I put the café up for sale."

"Nooo!" Roxy shouted. "You can't! I love the café. I love being a barista. You can't sell it!"

"I love Tiffany's too, Roxy," Rhonda said. "But I can't manage it alone anymore. And here's the thing…" Frank glanced over at Rhonda. She raised her eyebrows at him.

Frank nodded. "Tell them. Now's as good a time as any."

"Tell us what?" David and Roxy said together. Again, fear flickered across their faces.

"I've been out of sorts lately. You know that. My memory is jumbled up, I'm tired all the time, my back hurts after a few hours standing in the café, I'm irritable."

Roxy nodded the whole time Rhonda listed her symptoms. "Are you sick, Mom?" she asked. Tears sprang up in her eyes. "Is it something bad?"

Rhonda reached her hand out to Roxy. "Not sick. Not bad. Pregnant."

David choked. Roxy yelped.

"You're going to have a baby?" Roxy asked. "How…"

David elbowed Roxy. "How do you think, Rox?"

Roxy grinned. "I know how. But geez, I mean, Mom?" Roxy clapped her hands. "Far out! I finally get to be the big sister."

Rhonda said, "So things will be changing in several months. And, I have a plan of sorts. Let me tell you what I'm thinking."

48

Sunday, August 15, 2010

TIFFANY'S CAFÉ

GABE LEAPED FROM HIS F150, smacked the button to lower the garage overhead door, and climbed the interior stairs to his apartment, shucking his jacket on the way. He had half an hour before he was due at Tiffany's Café for Rhonda's Party Where Secrets Will Be Revealed.

As if secrets ever stayed secret in Cheakamus. Gabe had a solid idea of the secrets Rhonda was going to share. He didn't get to be a crackerjack P.I. without sources.

As soon as he pushed the apartment door open, he heard a soft thud and a petulant yowl. Doofus sat beside the recliner.

"Hey Doofus, did you have a good day?"

The cat yowled again and paced to his bowl on the kitchen floor. There he sat, staring at Gabe.

On his way to the kitchen cupboards, Gabe said, "I'm not even gonna ask what flavor you want." He emptied a tin of beef and gravy cat food into Doofus's bowl and watched the cat scarf it down, purring all the while. How did he do that, purr and eat at the same time?

Gabe returned to the cupboard and removed every tin of chicken-flavored cat food. Twenty-four in total. He placed them neatly inside an empty beer box, wrote "Congratulations!" on the side with a black marker, and taped the opening closed. Judge Quinn had told him what was going on in the upstairs space at Tiffany's Café—undoubtedly one of Rhonda's soon to be revealed secrets. This cat food would make the perfect gift.

He'd filed Judge Quinn under "sources, excellent." Also in that category were Roxy, who had blabbed to Jack, and Jack, who had blabbed to Gabe about secret number two: Frank and Rhonda were expecting a baby.

As he donned his gray cashmere sweater, the one that carried so many memories, Gabe smiled at Jack's comment after he'd spilled the baby beans. Jack had said, "It's almost the same as you and me, Gabe. The age difference I mean. Roxy and David are gonna be just as good as dealing with a bratty kid as you were."

He found a parking spot on Main Street, almost at the front door of *The Journal*. Parked next to him was a vintage blue and white Volkswagen Van with Alberta plates. The presence of that van confirmed what another excellent source, Rhonda, had told him two weeks ago. The third secret. The town's new police chief was an Albertan. Gabe also knew who owned that van. Amazingly small world.

He entered Tiffany's Café and went directly to his favorite booth at the back, where he plunked the cat food gift disguised as a case of beer on the tabletop. He didn't bother with his "out of order" sign because the din inside the café would overwhelm any screech from the toilet.

On his way to the rack of coffee thermoses, Gabe passed three old codgers sitting at a table with Mrs. Claus, aka Martha Stimmers. "Hey Martha," he said. "I hope you're keeping the Three Musketeers out of trouble."

The Viking tipped his mug in Gabe's direction. "Hey, sonny. We're planning a trip to Mexico this winter. Martha says she'll do the cooking if we do the fishing. Willie's coming along because if we leave him here on his own, he'll start selling Keith's Christmas trees again."

"Nice to see you fully recovered," Gabe said to Wilfred Stillwater.

Stillwater offered a sly smile. "Almost a hundred percent. But I think the coma did something to my head 'cause I don't remember selling any trees."

Not long after Gabe returned to his booth with his coffee, Harris entered the café. He was accompanied by his wife Kate and their year-old daughter Devon. Kate spotted Gabe, waved, and made her way over. "Can we join you?"

Gabe reached his arms out to Devon. "What do you think, sweetums? Should we let your parents sit with us? Or will it be just you and me, chowing down on ice cream sundaes?"

Devon squealed and bounced in her mother's arms.

When Kate handed the baby to Gabe, she said, "Devon says so long as she can have ice cream, Harris and I are welcome."

A few minutes later, Judge Quinn and Sergeant LeBlanc entered the café. LeBlanc was decked out in his red serge uniform. Gabe shot a quick glance at Kate and noticed the flush on her cheeks as she stared at the Mountie.

Rhonda put two fingers in her mouth and whistled. Immediately, all conversations ceased.

"Listen up!" Rhonda said. "I'm about to open the vault of secrets that several of us have been keeping for the last while. But before I do that, let's give a hand to Greta Rocque. She won the 'When Will George Eat Pie' pool by picking August second. She remembered I always offer free pies on our August civic holiday, and correctly guessed George could not resist."

When the applause died down, Rhonda continued.

"Right, secrets. First up, our very own RCMP Sergeant LeBlanc has news to share."

LeBlanc stepped forward. "I might be breaking the Mounties' rules about wearing the red serge, but Rhonda's party is a special event." He paused and cleared his throat. "Today is my last day with the force. Tomorrow the moving vans arrive, and Tuesday I begin my new career as chief of police in Eau Claire, Alberta."

The café was silent for a second and then people stood and clapped. Several whistled and chanted, "LeBlanc, LeBlanc, LeBlanc."

Gabe choked. Lucy had not said a word. He was mentally moving Lucy into the "sources, highly unreliable" file when the banshee toilet in the men's room screeched.

Rhonda said, "Gabe?" and flicked her hand toward the washrooms.

When Gabe returned from his task of sticking the "out of order" sign on the toilet stall, LeBlanc said, "I will miss Cheakamus. I won't miss trying to keep Gabrieli on the straight and narrow. You probably know he used to live in Eau Claire. The mayor of Eau Claire tells me that ever since Gabe moved here to Cheakamus, policing Eau Claire has been a cakewalk. I love cake."

Rhonda stepped forward again. "We'll miss you, Sergeant. But there will always be a slice of cake waiting for you here. Now, secret number two. There's been a lot of hammering above our heads for the last weeks. I'll let Judge Kathaleen Quinn tell you why."

Judge Quinn reached into a large tote bag she had placed at her feet when she first entered the café. When she faced the crowd again, she held Diva, her ragdoll cat. "I might also be breaking a rule or two by bringing Diva into the café. Diva and I hope you will all join us next Saturday for the grand opening of Lara's Loft Bookstore. Just upstairs from the café. Wally Mitchell has agreed to manage it for me and take care of Diva, who will be the resident cat while I am in court. She loves attention, so shop early, shop often!"

Gabe grinned. What bookstore cat didn't need to be fed?

He'd give the beer case of cat food to Judge Quinn before she left.

Rhonda said, "Secret number three. Mayor Chilton, please?"

Harris slid out of their booth at the back of the room and stood. "Most of you know the town has been searching for a chief to head our police force. Today I want to introduce you to the person we have convinced to do just that. Jennifer Sugar, formerly a sergeant in the Eau Claire police department."

Jennifer popped out from the kitchen and stood behind the counter. She smiled at everyone in the room and said, "I'm very much looking forward to this new job, even though I know Gabrieli lives here." She flashed a huge grin Gabe's way as the crowd erupted in laughter.

Gabe remembered that grin. It was the same one Jennifer flashed at him five years ago, when she tipped his canoe, and him, into Eau Claire Lake. Her payback for the disaster on their first and only date in high school fifteen years before that, when the mama skunk had sprayed Jennifer.

If the tables had been turned, he'd never have settled for merely tipping a canoe. But then again, he had anticipated payback of some kind for fifteen years before it finally arrived, and that waiting was worse than the dunking. Perhaps that had been Jennifer's plan all along.

Rhonda waved down the laughter. "Final two secrets coming up." At that point, Sergei Kravachenko emerged from the kitchen. Frank, Roxy, and David joined Rhonda at the front of the café.

"You all have enjoyed my guest chef Sergei's cooking for weeks now. I thought of selling the café…"

Gabe's heart plunged. Sell the café? She couldn't rock his world like that.

Everyone shouted, "Nooooooo!"

"Calm down," Rhonda said. "Then I realized I love

Tiffany's and the rabble who hang out here. But you know…" She took a deep breath and grabbed Frank's hand. "We, Frank and me, we're going to have another baby."

People shouted, "We know! Congratulations."

"You know?" Rhonda asked. "Honest to Pete, this town is a sieve." She laughed and then said, "But I bet you don't know that Sergei is going to be my partner in the business. We'll spell each other off. Same café. Same awesome attitude. Even better cooking."

Later in the afternoon, when the festivities were dying down, Gabe was alone in his booth babysitting Devon as her parents chatted with Sergeant LeBlanc. Jennifer Sugar slid onto the seat facing him. "Hey Gabrieli, what's shaking?

"You coulda told me you were in the running for the top cop job here when I saw you in Eau Claire."

"Didn't want to get your hopes up."

That she would get the job? Or that she wouldn't? Sometimes Sugar spoke in riddles.

"Sergeant LeBlanc told me policing Cheakamus has a few challenges," Sugar said. "But I figured after all the experience I had dealing with knuckleheads back in Eau Claire, this would be a snap."

"Hah! I haven't forgotten you called me that once upon a time."

Sugar shrugged and grinned. "You can't deny it fit the situation." She stopped smiling, leaned forward, and lowered her voice. "Are you still chasing Drake's mysterious killer?"

Gabe straightened in his seat. "When I can. But leads are slim. Why?"

"I might have a lead."

The hair on Gabe's arms rose. "Yeah?"

"Yeah. A friend on the Calgary police force told me a gang member looking to make a deal mentioned he could give them leads on several hired hits."

Gabe's heart skipped. "And one of the hits was Drake?"

Sugar smiled. "Got it in one."

Gabe mentally reviewed his calendar. Clear till Christmas.

The End

READ an extract from *The End Game,* the first novel in *The Gabrieli Mysteries*, to discover how Gabe, Doofus and Three ended up in Cheakamus. You can find the extract under "Extract from *The End Game.*"

Acknowledgments

I love Gabe Gabrieli and the people in his life. You'd think writing about them would be a solitary undertaking, but it's not. There are many people who helped me with *The Karma Murders.*

Talented writers like Karen Abrahamson, Marcelle Dubé, and Karen Sommerville pointed out plot holes, inconsistencies, and brainstormed ideas with me; Mark Marciniak, a fabulous cover designer took my brief description of the novel and created a knock-out cover; and Richard Feehan and Kathaleen Quinn (the real, live Kathaleen Quinn) supported the Sunshine Coast Writers and Editors Society by purchasing the right to name a character in the novel.

And of course, thanks to my husband John, who told me how a responsible law-abiding miner *should* shut down a mine so that I could create an irresponsible miner who thumbed his nose at regulations.

I'm also grateful to the organizations that support and promote writers, including Crime Writers of Canada, Sisters in Crime, and Author Nation, as well as all the readers who support authors by buying books and leaving reviews.

About the Author

Charlotte Morganti is an award-winning Canadian writer of crime fiction. She has been a burger flipper, beer slinger and a corporate finance/mining lawyer. Charlotte writes novels and short stories, ranging from gritty investigations to lighter capers. She usually sets her stories in small towns that miraculously harbor both villains (often cunning, occasionally inept) and the sleuths who pursue them.

The End Game, the first title in the *Gabrieli Mysteries*, was a finalist for the 2024 Crime Writers of Canada's Award of Excellence for Best First Crime Novel. *Breaking News: Local Heiress Dead*, won the 2025 Toby Award for Best Mystery, and the Sunshine Coast Writers & Editors Society's 2024 B.C. Book Award for Best Novel, Sunshine Coast Voices category.

Charlotte is a member of Sisters in Crime and Crime Writers of Canada.

Find out more, and sign up for Charlotte's newsletter, at https://charlottemorganti.com

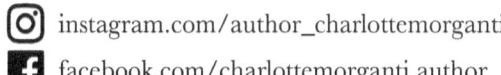 instagram.com/author_charlottemorganti
facebook.com/charlottemorganti.author

Extract from The End Game

Chapter 1

Rocky swiped a gloved hand across his forehead. One-thirty in the morning and balls-on-brass-monkeys-cold at this altitude, yet he was sweating like he was in a sauna. Not because he worried about the explosives. The Forcite was new and dry. Primo. If you want to steal something he always said, snatch the best.

No, what made Rocky's nerves jump was the gasoline. Explosives he could control. Gasoline—not so much. Ignition equaled instant flame. Plus, timing was vital. He couldn't risk someone investigating an explosion before the fire did its job, so the shack had to burn long and hot before he could set off the Forcite. Which meant he had to hang around, upping the risk he'd be seen.

He gulped air and told himself to calm down. Freaking out would only make him screw up. Again.

Following the Doc's master plan, Rocky tied several bundles of Forcite. He lowered some into drill holes on the exploration property and attached others to the drill tower. Then he unspooled thirty feet of fuse. Once he lit the fuse he'd have five minutes, more or less, to get the hell away before the exploration rig became pricey scrap metal.

He grabbed his two gas canisters, the glass bottle of gasoline and its wick, and hurried to the small wood building. Some core shacks were glorified carports, intended only to shelter mining samples from weather. Others, like this one, were sheds—walls, a door, windows—allowing the miner to catalog samples in comfort. Maybe have a sleep over.

Inside the shack, Rocky uncapped a gas can and poured its contents slowly, saturating the dead guy's clothing and body. Unfortunate it had come to this. For a braniac, the guy was okay. But too smart for his own good.

The fumes made Rocky's eyes water and his breath catch. Coughing, he ran outside. He filled his lungs with clean mountain air, held his breath, and entered the shack again. He sloshed gasoline over the wood racks, walls, and concrete slab before backing out, his lungs screaming. Outside, Rocky sucked in fresh air. When his chest stopped aching, he closed the door and poured the second canister of gasoline over the shed's exterior.

Finally, with the glass bottle in hand, he took up a spot several yards away, facing the shack's door. Here goes nothing, he thought, and lit the wick. It flared nicely. Imagining himself thirty years younger and back on the mound, Rocky wound up and fired the bottle at the door. Center of the strike zone. The bottle hit, the glass shattered, the gasoline ignited, and flames leaped and danced up the door and siding.

He grabbed the empty gas canisters, ran to the end of the fuse line and sat, staring at the fire. Nothing left to do but wait. Make sure everything burned nicely and Braniac became a crispy critter. Then he could light the fuse to the Forcite and leave.

The flames roared, devouring the shack's dry wood.

Chapter 2

Butt-sore and bleary-eyed, Gabe pulled into Cheakamus, B.C. midway through a sunny October morning. He needed coffee and breakfast. He angled his F-150 into a shady spot in front of a café called Tiffany's, one block past the traffic light on Main Street, and sat there. Not yet willing to shut off the engine.

Thinking.

It wasn't too late to turn tail, head home to the foothills and wide skies of Alberta.

Of all the places Gabe wanted to spend time, Cheakamus ranked lower than courtrooms. Lower than a salad bar. Barely above a church social. He had nothing against small towns, even when, like Cheakamus, they were clutched in a fist of mountains and had a wacko sabotaging nearby gold exploration sites. Gabe would even admit the place had a couple draws—his best friend Harris was the town's mayor, and recently Gabe's kid brother Jack had moved here. Two years ago, those positives would have been enough to convince Gabe that Cheakamus was worth checking out.

But not today.

Because Cheakamus was also where his horse Tornado

Callie now lived. And she brought memories of his darkest year raging to the surface.

He blew out a breath and rubbed his neck to ease the lengthy trip's accumulation of cricks. At the sound of rustling overhead, he raised his eyes to the open sunroof. Three feet above, give or take, a magpie perched on a branch, head cocked and one black eye peering down. Gabe knew The Frikkin Comedian, the *bête noire* who loved to mess with him, would seize the opportunity. He hit the sunroof button and the glass slid closed, a nanosecond before the bird shit splatted.

He reached to turn off the engine but hesitated, once more considering bailing out. Unbelievably, this upcoming commitment spooked him more than his worst case ever had. Until today only three things had ever terrified him: confined spaces, dealing with nutjobs, and the worry his marriage might really be over. And now, Gabe admitted as he stewed in his truck, perhaps a fourth: the thought of being some kid's godfather.

That was the trouble with a promise, especially one made to your oldest friend over a few double Scotches the night before his wedding. You'd likely regret it if called on to deliver. And when the friend was Harris Lancaster Chilton III, you'd definitely get that call. Gabe flicked the small silver spur on his key fob. Who'da thought Harris's wife Kate would go along with it?

He studied the bird-crap Rorschach on his sunroof. It looked exactly like a rubber chicken. "Sticks and stones," he said aloud.

A promise was a promise.

He shut off the engine and hauled his sore body from the truck. He was here. The christening was tomorrow. Hanging around Cheakamus for a couple days wouldn't kill him. And not even The Frikkin Comedian would mess with a baby's christening.

On the sidewalk, Gabe flexed his bum knee and watched a fire engine roar by, siren wailing. Then he opened the door to Tiffany's Café, releasing a blast of energetic voices and steamy air, laden with the aromas of bacon and real maple syrup. He pushed his way through the customers bunched by a commercial espresso machine, all of them watching a teenaged version of Katy Perry pull their shots. A sign inside Tiffany's entry directed: "Seat Yourself. No Fighting or Whining." Gabe cricked the right side of his lips upward and mentally filed the café under "Attitude, awesome."

He claimed the only empty stool at the counter, scanned the menu, and spotted an egg-sausage-pepper-cheese scramble named Ain't No Dude Ranch Special. After a nine-hour drive from Alberta, Gabe was heartened by the menu's guarantee the Special would kick-start his day.

While he waited for service, he placed a call to Jack. An automated voice informed him, "This mailbox is full. Please try again." Gabe sent a text: "Call me. I'm here and looking to see if I'm still taller than you."

A fortyish woman, who resembled the barista but was shorter and rounder at the edges, deposited cutlery on the counter. When Gabe glanced up at her, she studied him for a beat, her eyes lingering on his. "Welcome to Tiffany's," she said over the clacking espresso dispenser. "Famous for more than breakfast."

Gabe put his phone down and smiled. "Are you Tiffany?"

She guffawed. Throaty, joyful, and loud, momentarily quieting nearby conversations. "Kee-ryste. Do I look like a Tiffany? Nope."

He had to agree with her.

"I'm Rhonda Zalesko," she said.

"D. S. Gabrieli. Call me Gabe. Everyone does. I'll have your Dude Ranch Special. Hot sauce. Coffee, black."

"One Special coming up." She pointed to a rack of thermoses by the entrance. "Self-serve coffee over there."

He heaved himself from his stool and limped to the rack. While he studied the list of "Today's Oso Negro Beans" inked on the antique mirror above the thermoses, Gabe shifted his weight off his aching knee and fingered the small bandage on his forehead. The sutures were a week old and beginning to itch. His shiner, the same age as the stitches, formed a tasteful lime-green pouch beneath his right eye. Compared to last week, he looked refined and felt fit. Relativity was a brilliant concept.

He poured a large mug of Mudshark, advertised on the mirror as "swift, efficient, and deep," and reclaimed his stool. He'd barely sat down when his phone rang, the display flashing "H. Chilton."

"What's your ETA?" Harris said without preamble when Gabe answered the call.

"I'm here. Tiffany's Café. Apparently famous for more than breakfast."

"Pick you up outside in two minutes." Harris clicked off.

Gabe's stomach rumbled. He hit the call return button and sipped his coffee. The Mudshark was as complex as touted and more. When Harris answered, Gabe said, "Hang tight. I just ordered breakfast."

"Un-order it. There's been another explosion at an exploration site. This makes three. We gotta check it out. Now."

Chapter 3

THERE WERE times a guy could blow off a friend, but from the sound of Harris's voice, this wasn't one of them. Gabe tossed money on the counter, poured his coffee into a to-go cup, and was leaning against his truck's tailgate in forty-five seconds flat. His latest record for time taken to vacate an establishment voluntarily.

When he scanned the Saturday morning traffic on Main Street looking for a Jeep, he spotted Harris's bar, The Peak, diagonally across the road. Its dark green awnings and windows were clean, and the wood doors gleamed in the sun. A realtor's sign in one window caught his eye. It was crisp and bright, obviously a recent addition.

What the hell, the bar was for sale? Why hadn't Harris mentioned it? Perhaps excitement about the upcoming christening pushed the sale from his mind. Perhaps the legendary Chilton memory had experienced a momentary lapse. Perhaps Harris had stopped wearing bolo ties and driving red Wranglers. Not a chance.

Two rapid horn blasts drew Gabe's attention down Main Street, where a spotless red Jeep poked its nose out from behind a dusty dump truck. When the vehicle came even with

Gabe, Harris leaned out the driver's window, did a double-take and yelled, "Great shiner."

Harris spun a U-turn and stopped behind Gabe's truck. He jumped out and rushed over, the strings from his bolo tie swinging in time with his steps. Grinning, he shook Gabe's hand and smacked him on the back. "Good to see you, man. Walk into a fist?"

"Minor mishap at home."

Harris raised his eyebrows.

"Not worth getting into."

Harris's grin widened beneath his blond mustache. "I'd bet it is."

Gabe shrugged. "Nope."

Harris glanced at the F-150. "Yours?"

"Oh yeah." Gabe caressed the tailgate's pristine black paint and then nodded toward the bar. "What's up? You're selling?"

Harris grimaced. "Yeah. The sign went up last week. It's too much for us right now." He turned away. "C'mon. I'll drive."

When they buckled in, Harris stared at Gabe's jeans and boots. "Levi's, cowboy boots, and black F-150s. Some things never change."

"One thing hasn't changed for sure. I was hungry and looking for breakfast when I went into Tiffany's and now here I am, not three minutes later, outside the café, still looking for breakfast. Still hungry." Gabe sipped his coffee. "Why's that?"

"I want to get there before Jacobson hears about it and shows up to tell me any mayor worth his pay could put a stop to these explosions."

"Who's Jacobson?"

Harris blinked. "If you had visited just once in the five years since Kate and I moved here, you'd know."

"Life conspired against me," Gabe said. "But I'm here now, so tell me about Jacobson."

"Brief story? He owns the local paper and thinks he should be mayor instead of me."

They stopped at the traffic light at the River Road T-intersection. When the light changed, Harris turned left and followed River Road as it veered gently right onto a bridge spanning the Rocque River. As the Jeep rattled along the metal bridge deck, Harris said, "The sabotage is getting worse. This latest one is more than an explosion. Our fire chief says the bombers have added arson to their repertoire."

"And you dragged me away from my Dude Ranch Special because…?"

At the end of the bridge, Harris turned right onto Highway 41 and headed north. "A couple reasons. I'm counting on you, the former excellent lawyer turned successful PI that you are, to take one look at the scene and know who did it."

"Hah. You're correct about the former excellent lawyer bit. But as for the PI bit, I'm so successful, I gotta tend bar to pay the bills." Gabe stretched his arms above his head and yawned. "And just saying, I'm officially on vacation."

"I'm not asking you to work. Humor me and check out the scene? Something might jump out at you. Fresh eyes, y'know?"

After his long trip Gabe's eyes were far from fresh. But as they sped along Highway 41, he scanned the nearby treed slopes. Furrowed and folded like a much-loved grandmother's face, unlike the Rockies near Eau Claire, Gabe's hometown in Alberta. *His* mountains were hard rock, feisty, in-your-face peaks that shot abruptly from the dirt. "I don't see smoke. How far away is this place?"

"The smoke's long gone. The fire chief thinks it happened during the wee hours. Trail riders found the wreckage this morning. The site's not far west of town, but quite a hike up Rimrock Mountain, above a closed gold mine called the Evergold."

Gabe rubbed his neck. "When the first bombing hit the news in Alberta, the reports mentioned vandals. Is that your take?"

"One incident, I'd agree. But three explosions? All at exploration sites?" Harris groaned and flicked a quick sideways glance at Gabe. "This could give the town a notoriety it really doesn't need. I need help figuring it out."

The appeal of a challenging case and Gabe's natural inclination to help his friend almost made him blurt, "I'm in." Then he remembered his vow not to stay in Cheakamus longer than duty required. He said, "That's what the Mounties are for."

Harris's shoulders sagged. He turned left off Highway 41 onto Timberline Road, a skinny two-lane that wound up the steep hillside. "Welcome to Rimrock Mountain," he said, "home of some of the best trails around for ATVs and mountain bikes." As they approached a viewpoint looking south and east over Cheakamus, Gabe opened and closed his mouth to clear his ears. The southern horizon was a mere hint between two distant peaks. In the viewpoint's parking area, a fire truck displaying a "Cheakamus Volunteer Firefighters" emblem sat amid roughly a dozen vehicles and ATV trailers.

"Busy place," Gabe said.

"Deception Ridge Viewpoint. The primary access for trails."

Gabe glanced at the mountains facing the area. "Which one is Deception Ridge?"

"None of them. Back in the day the locals gave the name to this ledge, after a miner who was conned by his partner jumped to his death."

Harris turned right onto a narrow, overgrown logging road and gunned the Jeep along rutted switchbacks. Gabe grabbed the roll bar and grinned, exhilarated. Off-roading in Wranglers was what the Head Honcho had in mind when He created Heaven.

A couple minutes later Harris pulled into a small turnout and parked. He climbed out of the vehicle and pointed at a break in the wall of evergreen and birch that bordered the road. "C'mon, we walk from here."

Harris was halfway to the trees before Gabe extricated himself from the Jeep. When he caught up to Harris, he said, "You left your key in the ignition."

"No one's gonna take the car. This isn't the big city."

The understatement of the year. Gabe shivered in the hazy air. "Cold."

"Winter comes early in the mountains," Harris said. "It's been snowing in the high passes and on the ski runs for the last couple weeks."

Gabe zipped his leather jacket and jammed bare hands into his pockets, resolving to find a fireplace in town and park his body in front of it for the rest of the weekend.

They hiked a steep trail through firs and chalky birch skeletons to a field half the size of a major league ballpark. Small bushes and the occasional sapling dotted the field. Charred remnants of a building formed a black heap almost dead center of the clearing. Off to the side, a drill tower had been reduced to a twisted mess of black metal that leaned against a boxy, Hummer-sized engine.

Three firefighters stood in the middle of the debris, using crowbars and long-handled axes to separate burned wood from the heap. The smoky air almost masked an unsettling smell. Sulfur and something more—cloying, sweet.

Harris pointed out a fourth firefighter. "Our fire chief, Chester Ubrowski." He waved Ubrowski over and made introductions. The chief lifted a sweat-and-soot-stained hand at Gabe. "I'll do you a favor and not shake."

"What d'you know so far?" Harris said.

Ubrowski tipped his helmet back and wiped his face with a handkerchief. "Looks like they used dynamite on the drill tower, consistent with the other two bombings. Burning the core shack is a fresh twist—they used gallons of accelerant, probably gasoline. The debris is cool enough now to touch, so the fire likely started around midnight and burned itself out in a few hours." Ubrowski wiped his face again. "I have a nasty feeling about this one."

"You called the Mounties?" Harris said.

"On their way."

"How about Aldercott? Isn't this the site he's exploring?"

Ubrowski nodded. "Yep. We tried. Got voice mail."

A female firefighter shouted, "Chief."

The tightness in her voice made Gabe's stomach clench. When he added Ubrowski's uneasiness and the smell in the air to the mix, he knew, but didn't want to know, what lay under the debris. They moved closer and watched the firefighter use her crowbar to hook a piece of charred wood and fling it aside.

She removed two more blackened planks.

And uncovered a coal-black, twisted corpse.

End of Extract

Also by Charlotte Morganti

- The End Game, https://geni.us/The-End-Game

- Breaking News: Local Heiress Dead, https://geni.us/Local-Heiress-Dead

- Persimmon Worthing Short Mysteries, Volume 1, https://geni.us/PWShortMysteries-One

www.ingramcontent.com/pod-product-compliance
Lightning Source LLC
Chambersburg PA
CBHW031952240626
47153CB00003B/960